Restlessly Halina plucked a sketchbook and a few charcoal pencils from the table. She'd always enjoyed sketching, and now she had endless hours to hone her skill. Not that there was much to draw but craggy rocks and sand dunes.

A sudden commotion from outside her room had Halina stilling, the charcoal barely touched to the paper.

"You cannot, sir—" Ammar, one of the palace staff, exclaimed, and then the door was thrown open so hard it rocked on its hinges, swinging back and hitting the wall.

Rico Falcone stood there, dressed in desert camouflage fatigues, his sharp cheekbones flushed, his eyes glittering with fury. Halina's mouth dropped open and she found she couldn't speak.

"You," he said in a low, authoritative voice, "are coming with me."

Ammar burst in behind him. "You cannot take the princess."

"The princess is pregnant with my child," Rico returned evenly, the words vibrating with taut anger. "She is coming with me." His tone left no room for disagreement.

One Night With Consequences

When one night...leads to pregnancy!

When succumbing to a night of unbridled desire, it's impossible to think past the morning after!

But with the sheets barely settled, that little blue line appears on the pregnancy test, and it doesn't take long to realize that one night of white-hot passion has turned into a lifetime of consequences!

Only one question remains:

How do you tell a man you've just met that you're about to share more than just his bed?

Find out in:

A Night of Royal Consequences by Susan Stephens

A Baby to Bind His Bride by Caitlin Crews

Claiming His Nine-Month Consequence
by Jennie Lucas

Contracted for the Petrakis Heir by Annie West

Consequence of His Revenge by Dani Collins

Princess's Pregnancy Secret by Natalie Anderson

The Sheikh's Shock Child by Susan Stephens

The Italian's One-Night Consequence
by Cathy Williams

Look for more One Night With Consequences
coming soon!

Kate Hewitt

—

PRINCESS'S NINE-MONTH SECRET

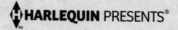
HARLEQUIN PRESENTS®

Recycling programs
for this product may
not exist in your area.

ISBN-13: 978-1-335-41966-8

Princess's Nine-Month Secret

First North American publication 2018

Copyright © 2018 by Kate Hewitt

Printed in U.S.A.

www.Harlequin.com

After spending three years as a die-hard New Yorker, **Kate Hewitt** now lives in a small village in the English Lake District with her husband, their five children and a golden retriever. In addition to writing intensely emotional stories, she loves reading, baking and playing chess with her son—she has yet to win against him, but she continues to try. Learn more about Kate at kate-hewitt.com.

Books by Kate Hewitt

Harlequin Presents

The Innocent's One-Night Surrender
Moretti's Marriage Command
Inherited by Ferranti

Conveniently Wed!

Desert Prince's Stolen Bride

One Night With Consequences

Engaged for Her Enemy's Heir
Larenzo's Christmas Baby

Secret Heirs of Billionaires

Demetriou Demands His Child

Seduced by a Sheikh

The Secret Heir of Alazar
The Forced Bride of Alazar

Visit the Author Profile page
at Harlequin.com for more titles.

To Laurie. Thank you for being such a fantastic editor! Warmest wishes, K.

CHAPTER ONE

IN THE END it was surprisingly easy to escape. Abdul, the royal bodyguard posted by the hotel suite's door, dozed off around ten o'clock, his head nodding onto his chest, and Halina Amari, Princess of Abkar, slipped by him on her tiptoes, holding her breath.

She'd never done anything like this before, never once tried to escape whatever narrow confines she'd been put in—although she'd certainly tested the boundaries and stretched her wings as much as she could, which was very little indeed. But tonight she wanted to fly.

This might be her last chance. The world was closing in, getting smaller and smaller thanks to her father—and Prince Zayed al bin Nur, her fiancé. The realisation of how close she'd come to being even more of a prisoner than she already was made her heart leap into her throat. And as for Olivia...

But she couldn't think about Olivia, not now, during her one bid for an evening's freedom. Halina hurried down the hall of the elegant luxury hotel in Rome towards the lift. Abdul stirred and she pressed herself against the wall. She could hardly believe it had been so easy, but why not? The door to their suite had been locked from the inside, the guard posted outside as a matter of form. Her mother had been trying to keep people out, not in. No one had expected her to escape. She could barely believe it herself.

The doors whooshed open and Halina stepped into the lift, her heart pounding, her palms slick. What was she *doing*? She'd spent every one of her twenty-two years hidden behind high walls—the palace, the convent school in Italy and then the palace again. Waiting, always waiting, for the fiancé she'd never met to regain his throne and become a suitable suitor. Waiting for her life to begin, or at least something to happen.

Three days ago, Zayed al bin Nur had mistakenly kidnapped Olivia Taylor, her sisters' governess and her school friend, thinking she was Halina herself.

Rumour was he'd married Olivia out in the desert before realising his grievous error. Zayed had sent a message to her father, assuring him that he had not in any way harmed Olivia, for which Halina was heartily relieved. But the whole episode had made her realise how precarious her own position was. How limited her own freedom. And it had infuriated her father, Sultan Hassan, who had sent Halina to Italy with her mother, away from Zayed's clutches.

Halina was glad for the escape; she'd never wanted to marry Zayed, a man she'd never even met, and she certainly didn't want to be kidnapped—

although she doubted her fiancé was fool enough to try the same trick twice. But the walls around her were closing in.

After this, her father would make sure she was even more restricted, more guarded, than she already was. And that was something Halina could not stand. After twenty-two years of waiting, she wanted to live…even if just for a night.

The lift doors opened and from the hotel's opulent ballroom she heard the tinkling sound of piano music and crystal, the low murmur of cultured voices. When she and her mother had arrived that afternoon, she'd seen the notice in the hotel's lobby about the private party, a charity function hosted by some CEO, a glittering event for all of Italy's richest and finest. Her mother had given Halina a sympathetic smile.

'One day, such parties will be for you,' she'd said, steering Halina towards the lift. 'When you are wed. But as for tonight, a quiet night in while we wait for your father's further instructions.'

Halina had never been to a proper party. Since she'd turned eighteen she'd attended a few dire state functions, endless banquets with fussy old dignitaries, but never a *party*. She'd never worn a cocktail dress, flirted or drunk champagne. And that was what she wanted to do tonight—to be normal just for a little while, a young woman having fun, enjoying life.

Of course, there were a few obstacles to be overcome. She'd managed the first—escaping her room.

She'd pleaded a headache and hidden in her room until her mother had gone to have a bath before making her getaway.

The second obstacle was clothes. She didn't have anything appropriate to wear. Fortunately the hotel had an upscale boutique, and after hurrying across the lobby Halina slipped into the elegant shop and picked the first suitable dress she saw—a knee-length sheath in black satin, simple, stark and very sexy. She found sheer stockings and high heels as well, and charged it all to her hotel room. She'd think about the repercussions later. Hopefully her mother would never look at the bill.

Holding the elegant bag with its embossed silver logo and thick cord handles, Halina snuck into the bathroom off the hotel's foyer and changed in a stall, her hands shaking as she stuffed her plain shift dress into the bag from the boutique. Was she really doing this? Was she *crazy*?

She'd always enjoyed pranks and dares, and had forever got into good-natured trouble at school. But this…this was something else entirely. If her mother discovered her…if her father found out… Halina trembled to think of their disappointment and wrath. Her parents were both genial, but they'd never had to deal with such direct defiance from her or her sisters. Still, she had to try. She'd just have to live with the potential consequences, whatever they were.

The door to the bathroom opened and Halina held her breath, one hand on the latch of her stall, fingers near to trembling. She couldn't be discovered now, not when her evening was just about to begin.

She heard the click of heels and from beneath the stall she saw the stiletto-shod feet of two women as they stood in front of the bank of sinks.

'Did you see him?' one of the women asked in Italian, in which Halina was fluent, as the other un-zipped her make-up bag. Halina peered through the crack in the stall's door and saw the women, sleek and elegant, their lips pursed and eyes narrowed as they gazed at their glossy reflections.

'Falcone? Yes, he's just arrived,' the other woman answered with a toss of her head. 'The man's *cold*. Sexy as anything, but with a heart of ice. He's fin-ished with his latest mistress, you know. Gave her the usual diamond bracelet as a payoff and now he's completely blanking her. She was crying her eyes out by the buffet.'

'That French supermodel? She didn't last more than a week.'

'They never do.' The other woman capped her lip-stick in one decisive movement. 'Would you fancy him?'

'Everyone fancies him. But would I *go* for him?' The woman tilted her head, considering. 'He must be fabulous in bed, based on everything I've heard, but I don't think I could warm up to someone that cold. One of his mistresses said that afterwards he always asks the woman to leave. And I mean, *right* afterwards. He's booting them out only seconds later.'

'There could be worse things.'

'And he insists on no personal questions at all. No asking, no answering, nothing. He just doesn't care.'

'But as long as you know that…'

'So it really would just be sex,' the woman finished with a sigh. 'And apparently that *is* amazing. That supermodel said she's been ruined for life, and it's only been a week.'

Halina's head whirled at the kind of gossip she'd never heard before. Whoever Falcone was, he sounded both appalling—and intriguing. Fabulous sex? She'd never even been kissed.

'Oh, well,' the first woman said as she zipped her bag up. 'Someone said he's already looking for his next mistress tonight—he doesn't like to have long in between paramours.'

'Mere minutes, it seems,' the other woman quipped. 'Well, it won't be me.' She sounded glum rather than determined.

With a swish of skirts and a click of heels the two women left the bathroom. Halina exhaled a huge sigh of relief. She was alone again—and it was time to make her own exit. She stuffed the bag with her own shift dress behind the toilet, hoping it would stay hidden for the evening until she was ready to return to her suite.

She hadn't quite figured out how she was going to return—would Abdul, her guard, still be asleep? And, if he wasn't, could she make something up about having taken a walk, gone for some fresh air? She'd just have to and hope Abdul—and her mother—bought her lie. This was her one night to shine, or at least twinkle a little.

Halina stepped out of the stall, her eyes widening at the sight of her reflection. The dress hugged her curvy figure, leaving little to the imagination. She'd never, ever worn something so flagrantly sexy. She'd never worn a dress so beautiful, so bare. She felt practically naked. The sheer stocking made her legs look long and slim, as did the sparkly black heels. She had no jewellery or make-up, and she'd have to leave her hair down, tumbled about her shoulders. She wouldn't look nearly as sophisticated as the women she'd just been spying on, but it would have to do.

One night. An hour, even. All she wanted to do was circulate among people, drink champagne, chat and maybe, *maybe*, flirt a little. And then she'd creep back to her bed. But for an hour—or two—she'd have fun. She'd live.

With her head held high, Halina walked out of the bathroom. She wasn't used to the heels and she stumbled for the first few steps before she got the hang of it, swinging her hips, sashaying a little. It buoyed her confidence, as did the admiring look from the man behind the concierge desk. She didn't even think he recognised her from when they'd checked in earlier in the day.

She followed the signs for the party and then paused as she saw a man on the door checking a guest list. She hadn't thought of that. The prospect of being turned away before she'd even put a toe inside the opulent ballroom made everything inside her shrivel with dismay and disappointment. She couldn't let that happen.

A couple glided past her, pausing in front of the man. Halina watched, nibbling her lip as they gave their names and he ticked them off his list. Another couple came by, and Halina watched as they followed the same procedure before going in.

Could she sweet talk her way in? She had a flair for the dramatic, but only in the safety of home or school. She'd never tried to charm a stranger, but she supposed she'd have to try.

Just then the man with the guest list caught her eye. He raised his eyebrows, managing to look both inquiring and a bit disdainful. 'May I help you, miss?'

Halina opened her mouth, her heart beating hard. 'Well…' she began, trying desperately to think of some credible reason why her name wasn't on the list but why she should still be allowed entrance to the party. 'As a matter of fact…'

The man's polite smile started to turn cool. 'Are you a guest tonight, miss…?'

Halina stared at him wretchedly. It was going to be over before it had even begun. Then she heard a voice from behind her, low and dark and rich.

'Yes, she is,' the man said. 'She's with me.'

Rico Falcone was looking for a woman, and he knew from the tightening in his gut that he'd found her. A startled gasp escaped the woman in question, her rosy lips parting as she whirled around to face him, dark hair flying about her shoulders in luxuriant waves and curls.

He'd caught a glimpse of her as he'd walked down the hall and his attention had been snagged immediately. A lush, curvy figure poured into a tight silk dress. Long, tumbling dark hair that she'd left loose and wild, like an open invitation. When she turned he saw dark-brown eyes widen, the colour of mahogany extravagantly fringed with soot-dark lashes.

'I…' she began in a breathy voice.

'Cara,' Rico purred, sliding a hand around her waist and enjoying the feel of his hip bumping hers. 'It was so good of you to wait for me.'

'I… I…' she stuttered again, looking shocked. Was she playing the innocent or was she just slow? She was obviously a gate crasher, so Rico would have expected her to play her part in this charade with a bit more alacrity. Never mind. He didn't bed women for their brains.

'Very good, Signor Falcone,' the man said, and ticked his name off the list, officious little nobody that he was. Rico moved into the room, his arm still around the woman's waist. She didn't resist, he noticed.

'Champagne, I think,' he murmured, and snapped his fingers. A waiter hurried forward and Rico plucked two glasses from the proffered tray before handing one to his next mistress. He'd already decided on that, although he didn't think she'd last too long. They never did. 'So. You obviously don't have an invitation to this party, but what is your name?' It was just about the only information he required of her.

'H— Lina,' she said, her fingers clenched tight around the stem of her glass.

'Lina?' He arched an eyebrow. 'You sounded as if you were going to say something else.'

She smiled sweetly, her eyes flashing dark fire, intriguing him. 'Lina will do for you.' So she had some spirit. He liked that, as long as she didn't start getting notions, thinking she could control him. Make him care. A few of the women he'd bedded had made that error, and it had been very tedious indeed. He'd had to make short work of them, when he would have enjoyed their attentions for a little bit longer.

'Lina,' he repeated, letting the syllables slide around in his mouth. 'And why were you so desperate to attend a party that you weren't invited to?'

She cocked her head, her smile teasing, her eyes alight, although he sensed a surprising nervousness underneath. 'What girl doesn't want to have fun?'

'Right answer,' he murmured, and clinked her glass. Her smile deepened, revealing a delightful dimple in one cheek, and she took a sip of her champagne.

'Oh, it's delicious!' she exclaimed, and he couldn't help but laugh.

'You almost sound as if you haven't tasted champagne before.'

She gave him a haughty look. 'Of course I have,'

she said, and then, as if to prove the point, she drained her glass.

'Time for another, I think,' Rico said, and summoned a waiter with one imperious gesture. This woman, this Lina, was fascinating. Gate-crasher, definitely. Gold-digger as well, he was quite sure. He didn't mind, though; as long as women were upfront about what they wanted—as he was about what he didn't—the arrangement was usually satisfactory. He felt the tingle through his body of attraction and, yes, desire as he looked at her. Tonight, he hoped, was going to be very satisfactory.

She was certainly lovely, and unabashedly sexual with her tight dress and tumbled hair. She hadn't bothered with make-up or jewellery, as if she had no need for extra frippery for what was, after all, a very basic transaction. She'd come to this party looking for fun, and quite possibly a protector. Rico intended it to be him, at least for a short while.

He took another flute of champagne from the proffered tray and handed it to her. *'Cin cin,'* he murmured, and she smiled.

'Cin cin.' They'd been speaking Italian, and hers was flawless, although Rico suspected it was not her first language. He wondered what was. There was a faintly exotic cast to her features, her slightly tilted eyes and golden skin. He had no intention of or interest in asking her such questions or learning more about her. He'd long ago found that women started expecting things, emotional things, when he asked

them even the most basic of questions. So he didn't. And he made sure they didn't ask any of him, either.

'Lina,' he said. 'This party bores me. Do you want to go upstairs?'

Surprise flashed through her eyes and her tongue darted out to moisten her lips, causing another painful arrow of desire to knife through him. 'Upstairs?'

'Yes, upstairs. I have the penthouse suite.' He let his mouth curve in a lazy smile. 'I think it would be a great deal more comfortable up there, and the champagne is of a far better vintage.'

'I don't even know your name,' she protested, her cheeks flushing. She looked uncertain but also excited. Perhaps he'd been a bit too abrupt. He was getting tired of the same old niceties.

'Rico,' he said, although he was quite sure she knew who he was. Everyone here did. 'I'm the CEO of Falcone Enterprises.'

'Falcone…' Recognition flashed in her eyes.

'You've heard of me, then.'

'Yes, in the bathroom just now.' Lina bit her lip, looking both guilty and amused. 'Two women were talking about you.'

'Were they?' Rico arched an eyebrow. 'Women's gossip in a bathroom—I can imagine what they said, and I assure you, it's all true.'

Her eyes rounded. 'All of it?'

Rico didn't even hesitate. 'All of it,' he drawled, and Lina let out a hiccupping laugh. She had, he noticed, already finished her second glass of champagne.

'They said you were cold. A heart of ice...'

'Pejorative, but essentially true.'

'Oh?' Lina tilted her head, her eyes sparkling, a small smile curving her lush mouth. 'How are you so cold, then?'

Rico took a sip of champagne, considering. 'I'm matter-of-fact,' he stated, deciding as always that bold honesty was by far the best policy. 'I don't dress up what is essentially a physical and very satisfying transaction.' He met her curious and impish gaze with a direct challenge in his own eyes, and he watched with pleasure as colour flared in her cheeks and her lips parted soundlessly.

'Do you mean...?' she began, and Rico cut her off.

'Yes,' he said. 'I do mean.'

She shook her head slowly, her pupils dilated, her cheeks still wonderfully pink. 'They said something else in the bathroom.'

'Did they?' Although he affected a bored drawl he realised he was interested. He wanted to know what Lina had heard, what preconceptions she might have of him.

'They said...they said...' She licked her lips, making his libido take a little leap. 'They said you were fabulous at sex.' She let out a little laugh, seeming almost incredulous that she'd admitted such a thing. Rico's mouth curved into a wicked smile.

'Also true.'

She laughed again, shaking her head, seeming embarrassed, almost shy. Was it an act, a rather obvious and unneeded attempt to snag his interest? A woman didn't pour herself into a sexy dress and try to gate-crash the party of the year without having some brash confidence and bold hopes.

'So?' Rico demanded in a low, sensual voice. He was tired of chitchat, of waiting. 'Shall we go up-stairs?'

'Upstairs…'

'To my suite. A bottle of champagne is waiting.' It always was.

'I… I don't…'

Annoyance flickered through him. He didn't have time for this. Rico stretched out one hand and slid his fingers through hers, enjoying the shower of sparks that fired through him at that slight touch. He'd made the right choice, he was sure of it. 'Well?' he murmured. 'Are you coming…or not?'

CHAPTER TWO

HALINA COULDN'T THINK. From the moment Rico Falcone had rescued her from the box-ticking bouncer, she'd been ensnared. Bound body and mind by the sensual charisma of the man standing in front of her, so arrogant and self-assured and so very, very attractive.

She had limited experience of the opposite sex, and she had no experience whatsoever of the kind of man who stood in front of her now, one dark slash of an eyebrow arched, his mobile mouth curved into a smile of supreme self-confidence, his body radiating pure, muscular, sensual power.

'Are you coming with me?' he asked, and there was a note of challenge in his voice, as well as a hint of impatience. Halina hesitated. She shouldn't go with him, of course, this man whom she knew, from both gossip and his own gorgeous mouth, was a cold womaniser. A man who was fabulous at sex.

Not that she had any intention of having sex with him, of course. Her virginity was a point of honour, as well as a prized asset. As a princess of a desert kingdom, her chastity was of utmost importance. She'd never even *touched* a man before tonight.

But why did this have to be about sex? All she wanted was to drink champagne, perhaps even be kissed…

It was hard to resist such a beguiling invitation. And he was quite the most perfect specimen of a man she'd ever seen—dark hair cut close, silvery grey eyes that flashed like sunlight on metal as he remained with his hand outstretched, fingertips gliding along hers, his tall and powerfully built body encased in a top-end tuxedo, the crisp white shirt and black fitted jacket the perfect foil for his dark hair and grey eyes, his swarthy skin.

From the corner of her eye Halina saw the two women she'd glimpsed in the bathroom shooting her speculative and frankly envious glances. No matter what they'd said to each other, they wanted this man…this man who, improbably, *impossibly*, seemed to want her.

'Yes,' she said, flinging the word out the way a knight would fling down a gauntlet. It felt like a challenge, a dare, completely reckless but also brave. 'Yes, I will.'

'Excellent.' His fingers tightened on hers, causing a fizz of fireworks to go off in her belly. She was already feeling light-headed from two glasses of hastily drunk champagne, imbibed to steel her nerves. Now she felt utterly overwhelmed by the sheer, lunatic magic of the situation—she, the innocent Princess in her ivory tower being lured upstairs by the most magnetically sexual man in the world, never mind this room. *And he wanted her.*

Taking a deep breath, Halina followed Rico down the hall, away from the party, determined not to panic or even doubt herself. A little bit of flirting, another glass of champagne, maybe a kiss…and then she'd leave. Of course she would. And she wouldn't think about her mother, or Abdul, the sleepy bodyguard, and certainly not her father the Sultan who would be both furious and heartbroken to know she'd dared to go this far, never mind what she might get up to once they were in Rico's suite.

One night. One adventure. That was all she wanted, all she was asking for. Surely it wasn't too much?

Rico stabbed the button for the lifts and the doors whooshed open. Still holding her by the hand, he drew her inside, then the doors closed and they were alone, soaring upwards.

'So what made you decide to crash the party tonight?' he asked in a lazy voice. Halina tried not to blush. So it had been obvious that she hadn't had an invitation.

'An impulse decision.'

'Some of the best decisions are borne from impulse.'

'Are yours?' she asked. She was so nervous and hyper-aware of him that she wondered if he could see the hectic, urgent thud of her heart from beneath her dress. She resisted the urge to wipe her damp palms down its sides.

'My impulses are borne of instinct,' Rico answered. 'So they're always right.'

She laughed, incredulous and a little bit amused by his arrogance, despite her nerves. 'Is there anything you're insecure about?'

Something dark flashed across his face, so quickly that Halina almost missed it. She couldn't decipher what it was. Then his expression evened out and he smiled, his lips curving, showing a flash of very white, very straight teeth. 'No,' he answered. 'There isn't.'

The doors opened straight into the penthouse suite of the hotel, the one her mother had demanded but which the concierge had regretfully informed her was already booked. What kind of man was Rico Falcone, that the hotel had turned away even a queen?

'So, where's this wonderful champagne?' Halina asked as she stepped into the suite, her heels clicking the black marble floor. The space stretched on into the darkness, the only light coming from the floor-to-ceiling windows overlooking the city.

Rico threw her a darkly amused glance. 'Are you quite certain you want another glass?'

Surely he wasn't going to treat her like a child? Halina lifted her chin. 'Why wouldn't I?'

'I don't want you drunk when I make love to you.'

Everything inside her trembled, her internal organs reduced to a plateful of jelly. 'Who says you're going to—to make love to me?' Halina demanded with far more bravado than actual courage. An image slid through her mind like a sensuous snake—body entwined with body, candlelight gleaming off satin sheets—and a current of desire zinged through her, twanging all her senses, every nerve.

'I do,' Rico replied baldly as he retrieved a bottle of champagne chilling in a silver ice-bucket by a pair of white leather sofas. 'Why else would you have come up here with me?'

Nerves clamoured in her belly. Was she in over her head? The answer was obvious—of course she was. Yet she didn't want to leave. Not so soon, not yet. 'For the champagne, of course,' Halina quipped as she strolled through the sweeping living area of the suite towards the floor-to-ceiling windows that overlooked the Eternal City, its ancient, crumbling buildings now awash with moonlight.

'At least on that I can oblige.' With a satisfying pop he pulled the cork from the bottle and then filled two glasses right to the brim before handing one to Halina. She took a sip, relishing the crisp taste of bubbles on her tongue, and definitely needing the Dutch courage. *What now?*

'You really shouldn't be quite so arrogant,' she said as she lowered the glass. Her palms were slick and her heart thudded but she managed to hold his sardonic gaze. Just.

'Oh? Why shouldn't I?'

His utter, unapologetic confidence stunned her. She admired it too, because although she knew she could seem confident to her school friends or sisters, playing to familiar crowds with her trademark drama and humour, when it came to the real world she had nothing on this man. Nothing at all.

'It's not a particularly appealing trait,' she said at last.

'I disagree.'

His self-assurance was like a brick wall, high and wide, impossible to cross or find a chink in. Still, for some perverse reason, she tried. 'So you think it's an asset? Being so ridiculously self-assured?'

He shrugged, as if the answer was so apparent the question should not have even been asked. 'Of course.'

'Why? How?'

'Because there is a basis for it. I am the way I am because I know what I'm doing and, more importantly, I know what I want and I go after it.' His eyes flashed, a glint of silver like moonlight flashing off the blade of a knife. 'And do you know what I want right now, Lina?'

She swallowed. Hard. Excitement licked along her veins like the most dangerous fire. 'What?'

'You.'

Before she could form the words for a semi-coherent reply he'd crossed the room, swallowing up the space in a couple of strides, and plucked the champagne flute from her nerveless fingers. She opened her mouth to protest—she hadn't finished her drink—but then his hands were on his shoulders, warm and so very sure, and he was kissing her.

Her very first kiss, and it felt like diving head-first into ice-cold water, a shock to her entire system. She stiffened underneath the onslaught of his persuasive mouth, the sudden intimacy of it, even as heat exploded in her centre and stars shot from behind her eyes. Her knees buckled and she felt Rico smile against her mouth as he gauged her obvious and overwhelming response to him.

She clutched at the slippery, satiny lapels of his tuxedo jacket, lost in the sensation of his mouth on hers. Were all kisses like this? Did you always feel as if you were drowning, caught up in a whirlpool of pleasure, every sense singing? She'd never experienced anything like it, and all she knew was that she wanted more. Much more.

Her mouth opened under his and she stood on her tiptoes, straining to reach more of him. Feel more of him. Her breasts pressed against his chest and created even more arrows of sensations sizzling through her, making her whole being burn.

Rico slid his hands from her shoulders to her waist, anchoring her against him so her hips nudged his and she felt the hard throb of his arousal against her, shocking her to her core and thrilling her too. Even she, in her innocence, knew what *that* was. As much as it thrilled her, it also made a ripple of terror go through her. What was she *doing*? And did she want to stop?

Rico spread his fingers across her hip, each lean digit creating a burn even through her dress as if he were branding her by his touch. She was so achingly conscious of every part of him, from the hard planes of his chest and thighs to the sure movement of his mouth and the delightful press of his hands. He was everywhere on her, yet she still wanted more, a delicious and insistent ache of need starting at her centre and spreading outwards, right to her fingertips.

She felt so much, she was afraid she might combust, burst into flames right in front of him. How did people experience this and *live*?

Then, quite suddenly, Rico tore his mouth from hers and took a step away, raking his hands through his hair before dropping them to his sides. Colour blazed along his blade-like cheekbones and his breathing was ragged. He was, it seemed, as affected as she was, or almost, and that was an incredible thought.

Halina's knees wobbled and she grabbed onto a nearby table to steady herself. She felt the absence of him like a physical thing, everything in her all at once turning empty, cold and aching. For a little while she'd felt so gloriously alive. She couldn't let it end so quickly. She couldn't let it end at all.

Because she knew then, no matter how inexperienced and nervous she was, she wanted more. Needed it. She wasn't done with Rico…and she prayed he wasn't done with her.

Rico gazed at Lina thoughtfully, trying to ignore the hectic thud of his own heart. He'd been far more affected by her clumsy kisses than he liked to admit, even to himself. Even in love-making, in the highest heights of his pleasure, he kept his control. To lose it would be another form of weakness, one he despised. He would not be a slave to any emotion, whether it was love or its poorer but equally powerful cousin, lust. He'd decided that a long time ago, when he'd watched someone walk away from him and felt his heart break. *Never again.* Never again would he allow someone to break something inside him. He wouldn't even allow himself to be affected... at all. Never would he give in to the weakest emotion of them all, the torment of love.

And as for Lina... He let his gaze sweep over her, noting her flushed cheeks and swollen lips, her ink-dark, wavy hair falling in tumbling waves over her shoulders. Her breath shuddered through her, and artlessly she pressed one hand to her pounding heart. She was just as affected as he was, and she wasn't even trying to hide it. He didn't think it had even *occurred* to her to hide it, to hide anything, and that made her very different from the women he usually bedded.

Those women were beautiful and hard in a sharply glittering way, as determined to get his money as much as they were eager to get into his bed. He gave them pleasure, of that he was certain, but they didn't respond as Lina just had—trembling and eager, unrestrained and artless, seeming to crave him just for him...which was an intoxicant in and of itself.

'What is it?' she asked, her voice a breathy whisper. 'Why are you looking at me like that?'

'How am I looking at you?'

'As if I'm a puzzle you're trying to solve.'

He laughed; he couldn't help himself. She was absolutely right and he wasn't used to that kind of perception, especially from a potential bed partner. 'Yes,' he said. 'That is how I'm looking at you. You intrigue me, Lina.' More than she should. He didn't want to be interested in the women he bedded, beyond their capabilities in that particular department.

Yet something about Lina, her utterly unrestrained response, made him pause. And then wonder. Because, he realised, she seemed the one thing he felt he'd never been, at least not since he'd been nine years old and realised that promises could be broken and dreams shattered. Easily.

What had given him pause just now was that Lina seemed innocent. And innocence was a quality in his bed partners he definitely did not want. He'd had enough dreams broken not to want to break anyone else's, which was why he was so upfront about his relationships, if he could even call the sexual transactions he enjoyed such a thing.

'I don't think I'm that complicated, really,' she said on a laugh, but the sound wobbled and she bit her lip, increasing Rico's curiosity…and his unease. Why was she acting as if this was all so *new* to her?

'Tell me what you were doing tonight at the party,'

he said abruptly. Her eyes widened in surprise at the sudden change of subject.

'Trying to get into it,' she answered with a shrug. 'I didn't have an invitation, as you realised.'

'Do you do that often? Try to crash parties you aren't invited to?'

'Not…that often,' Halina said, keeping his gaze, but clearly with effort.

'But why that party?' Rico pressed. 'And why did you want to get into it so badly?'

A frown crinkled her forehead and something flashed in her eyes, something like unease. She was hiding something. But what? He'd already assumed she was a gold-digging mistress-in-expectation. What could she possibly be hiding that would bother him?

'Why not that party?' she challenged. 'It looked fun.'

'Were you hoping to meet someone in particular?'

She shrugged. 'I was hoping to have fun.'

Rico swung away from her, annoyed as much with himself for pressing the point as he was with her for her non-answers. What did he care why she'd shown up tonight or what her motives were? What did he care at all? He never had before. And he wouldn't now.

She was here in his suite for a reason. When she'd kissed him, as clumsily as she had, it had been with a genuine, eager desire. She was willing and so was he. That was all that mattered, surely?

And yet…it was almost as if she'd never been

kissed before. She'd been so unrestrained, so open, and it had been that seeming innocence that had enflamed him. Yet surely she couldn't be as innocent as all that? Surely she wouldn't be in his suite now if she was?

'I've drunk all my champagne.'

Rico turned to see Lina clutching her glass, a determined tilt to her chin. She held it out and after a second's pause he reached for the bottle and poured her another glass, the fizz foaming over the top and onto her hand. She laughed and licked off the droplets, a move that seemed as thoughtless and uncomplicated as everything else she did. If it had been another woman, the kind of woman he was used to, he would have thought it a planned part of an attempt to ensnare him. Not that he could ever be ensnared.

'Cin cin,' she said again, a note of defiant bravado in her voice, and she lifted her glass to drink. Rico watched her, noting the sinuous movement of her throat as she swallowed, wondering yet again what was making him hesitate.

'Cin cin,' he answered automatically, even though he'd discarded his glass already. Slowly Lina lowered her glass, her eyes wide and dark above the rim as she stared at him.

'I… I should probably go now,' she said, and that surprised him even more. Was she playing hard to get? Or did she really mean it? And should he let her, considering how uneasy this whole exchange was making him feel? He felt strangely reluctant to watch her walk away, which was irritating and alarming in itself.

'Do you want to go?' he asked starkly.

She paused, her tongue darting out to dab a drop of champagne sparkling on her lips. Her gaze was wondering and transfixed as she slowly, so slowly, shook her head. 'No…no, I don't. But I probably should.'

'Should? Why?'

'Because you're a dangerous man, Rico Falcone.' She set the glass on a side table. 'And you're way out of my league.'

More honesty that took him by surprise. He wasn't used to such unvarnished truth. 'I'm not so dangerous if you know what to expect.'

'Which is?'

'A wonderful time and then a farewell.' He was absolute about that. He would never be left again, never watch someone walk away, leaving his heart in pieces. No, he would watch whomever it was walk away, a smile on his face because he was in control. He was always in control.

'Ah.' She nodded slowly. 'Just like the women said.'

'Those women in the bathroom?'

'The very same.'

He walked towards her, a long, loose-limbed, lazy stroll. 'Forewarned is forearmed, or so they say.'

'They said you kicked women out of your bed in rather indecent haste.'

'I suppose it depends on whom you ask.'

He stood in front of her so he could feel the heat

coming off her, the desire. Her body trembled. He felt as if they were both on the edge of a glorious precipice; all it would take was for one of them to take that first tumbling step.

'I really should go.' Her voice was soft.

'Don't play games with me, Lina.' He met her gaze; her lids were half-lowered in dark challenge. 'I abhor any kind of dishonesty. If you want to go, go.' He swept one arm towards the lift. She didn't move, and if she had he didn't know what he would have done. Stopped her? Persuaded her to stay in any way that he could? Maybe. Probably.

But Lina stayed still, her gaze darting from the lift back to him. 'This is madness,' she whispered.

'Why?'

'Because…because I don't even know you. And you don't know me.'

'We know enough.'

'For you, maybe.' She closed her eyes briefly. He had the sense that she was battling with herself, and he wondered why it was such a momentous decision. She'd come to the party. She'd come upstairs. Was she going to cling to some outdated remnant of morality now? Still, it felt bizarrely important not to push her. This would be a decision she'd make on her own, though God help them both if she walked away now.

Then Lina opened her eyes. Stared him straight in the face. Took a deep breath and spoke. 'I'm staying.'

CHAPTER THREE

HALINA WASN'T SO innocent that she didn't know what she was agreeing to. Her heart tumbled in her chest and excitement zinged through her veins because, no matter how crazy this was, how nervous she felt, she wanted this. A lifetime of humble obedience and duty to her royal family and it had all shattered to broken pieces with Prince Zayed's foolish, desperate act. She would not marry him now; she might not marry anyone. So why not take one night? One night for herself, for pleasure? She'd deal with the consequences later. Maybe she'd be lucky and there wouldn't be any.

'Are you sure?' Rico's dark gaze searched hers, his voice a rumble in his chest. Halina had the feeling it was not a question he asked often. Did he know how innocent she was? Had he any idea that he was her first kiss, her first everything? Halina had no intention of telling him. She had a gut instinct that such lack of experience would horrify and perhaps even repel him. She wasn't like his usual women. Even in her inexperience, she knew that.

'Yes, I'm sure.' The words trembled through her

and part of her, quite a large part, wondered what on earth she was doing. Losing her innocence, her prized virginity, to a man who had made it clear he had no expectations, no desires, beyond sex. Fabulous sex.

But perhaps that was better. This didn't have to be complicated. There would be no entanglements. And after a lifetime of waiting she wanted, *needed*, something finally to happen. To be the author of her own destiny, if only for an evening. Even if it ultimately led to heartbreak, or at least disappointment.

'Lina.' Rico's voice was rough. 'If you're sure, come here.' Her eyes widened but then she obeyed, walking towards him on trembling legs so she was standing before him. 'Take off your dress.'

Her heart was thudding so hard it hurt. Was he really going to ask her to do that right *now*? She swallowed hard and Rico's gaze seemed to burn into hers, his eyes like molten silver as he waited for her to obey his command.

'Well?' One eyebrow lifted arrogantly. This was a test, a dare; if she didn't do it, he would call her bluff. Accuse her of inexperience, and maybe even send her away. Taking a deep breath, her gaze never leaving his, Halina reached behind her and tugged the zip down her dress.

As the dress slithered off her shoulders, leaving her bare to the waist—her breasts encased in a serviceable white bra rather than the sexy lingerie she would have preferred—Halina could hardly credit she was doing this. Was it the champagne that lent the recklessness to the moment, or was it the urgency she felt? Or was it the man himself, Rico Falcone, his body radiating the most powerful sexual charisma Halina had ever experienced?

The dress pooled around her waist and Halina lifted her chin, resisting the impulse to cover herself. 'Well?' she demanded, and thankfully her voice didn't waver. 'Take off your shirt.'

With a low husk of laughter, Rico undid his tie and then the studs of his tuxedo shirt, tossing them aside heedlessly so they clattered onto the marble floor. He shrugged out of his jacket and shirt so his chest was bare and magnificent, his skin gleaming like bronze satin stretched over powerful muscles, the dark hair sprinkling his impressive chest veeing down to the waistband of his black trousers.

'Touch me,' he said softly, and it felt more like a plea than a command, surprising her, because for a moment Rico Falcone didn't seem arrogant. Gently she placed her hand on his chest, the dark, crisp hairs a sensual abrasion against her palm. His skin was warm, the muscles hard and flexed, and she felt the steady thud of his heart beneath her palm.

Rico encircled her wrist with his fingers, holding her hand there, against him. Neither of them spoke; the only sound was the ragged draw and tear of their breathing. Halina had never felt so close to a human being before, connected in a way that felt both intimate and intense.

Rico's fingers tightened on her wrist, and then he

drew her slowly towards him so her hips and breasts pressed against him. The feel of his body in such close contact with hers made a thrill run through her, as if a live wire ran right through her centre and Rico's touch was the electric current.

He dipped his head, his mouth hovering over hers, their breaths mingled, everything suspended. Halina's eyes fluttered closed, waiting for his kiss, but then she opened them again when he remained where he was, his lips barely brushing hers.

'Rico...?'

Whatever he saw in her questioning gaze seemed to satisfy him, for in one swift movement he drew her even more closely to him, his hands on her hips, shrugging her dress down to her ankles as his mouth plundered hers with soft yet determined persuasion.

Halina brought her hands up to his head, her fingers threaded through his short, dark hair, her nails grazing his skull as she surrendered herself, body and soul, to that one endless kiss that demanded everything from her.

Her mind was a blur of sensation as Rico backed her towards the corridor that led to the suite's bedrooms; she stepped out of her dress, stumbling slightly in her unfamiliar heels, and when she did he swept her up in his arms as if she were an armful of feathers and, with her curled against his chest, he strode into the bedroom.

The room was swathed in shadows and moonlight as Rico laid her on the bed. She was dressed only in her stockings and plain bra and pants, and she felt shy but not uncertain as she lay sprawled on the black silken sheets for his thorough inspection.

And inspect he did, standing above her as he slowly unbuckled his trousers and then shucked them off so he wore nothing but a pair of navy silk boxer shorts that did little to hide the impressive evidence of his masculinity.

'You are very beautiful.' The words were stark and sincerer because of it. Rico was not a man to flatter; he was merely stating a fact. And Lina could tell by the silver blaze of his eyes that he meant every simple word.

'Thank you,' she whispered. Rico stretched out alongside her, the sinewy muscles of his body rippling with the easy movement. Halina held her breath as he hooked his fingers around the edge of her tights and tugged them downwards.

Her breath came out in a restless shudder as the tips of his fingers brushed against her sensitive core, igniting sensations she'd barely felt before. He tugged the tights lower, down her thighs, leaving fiery trails of sensation wherever his fingers brushed until he'd got rid of them completely and tossed them aside.

He loomed above her, his hands braced by her shoulders and his knees on either side of her hips. She felt caged by his body, but it felt protective rather than threatening, thrilling in a way she could barely articulate even to herself. She had no idea what he was going to do next.

Then he lowered his mouth and pressed a kiss to her navel, his tongue flicking inside her belly button and making her cry out in surprised pleasure. The cry turned to a moan as his mouth moved lower. Surely he wasn't going to…?

But he was. His breath fanned hotly on her underwear before he hooked his finger through the top of it and slid it down her legs so it went the way of her tights. She was bare and exposed before him, and it made her both tense and strain in expectation, incredulous and waiting, a little bit embarrassed and yet so eager.

Her body arched off the bed as he pressed his mouth to her centre, the feeling so intimately invasive that her mind blurred into nothing but sensation. His tongue flicked among her folds, seeming to know exactly what touch and pressure would make her writhe mindlessly, her body attuned to the exquisite pressure building within her.

'Rico.' His name was a moan, a plea. Her hips bucked with the restless ache inside her that she desperately needed to be assuaged. 'Rico.'

He lifted his head, laughing softly, and then he slid his hands under her bottom, lifting her up so he had even greater access to her most intimate self. She felt too crazed with desire and need now to feel embarrassed or exposed, wanting only more from him.

And he gave it, his mouth plundering her centre until she felt as if she were shattering inside, breaking apart into glittering pieces, her hips arching under his knowing touch as her cries rent the still, taut air.

She'd never known anything like it, had never had such an experience so intimate, so intense, so overwhelming.

Rico rolled on top of her, braced on his forearms, his breathing ragged. 'Is it safe?' he demanded in a ragged voice and Halina blinked up at him, still dazed by an experience she could only describe as completely life-changing.

Safe? What, she wondered hazily, was safe about this? She was risking everything, including her very soul, by being here with him. It wasn't remotely safe. But she sensed that if she said as much Rico would exercise the incredible self-control she instinctively knew he had and roll off her, tell her to go. Their night would be over, and she couldn't bear the thought.

'Yes, it's safe.'

With a grim smile of satisfaction curving his features, Rico nodded, then Halina gasped as she felt him start to slide inside her. Her fingernails pierced his shoulders as she braced herself for what felt like a complete onslaught, an invasion of everything she was.

Before she could accept the discomfort and adjust to it, Rico stopped. His expression was one of complete and utter astonishment.

'You are a *virgin*?'

* * *

She couldn't be. Rico gritted his teeth, sweat breaking out on his brow as he held himself above Lina, calling on every shred of self-control he had to keep himself from sinking inside her velvety depths as he longed to do.

Lina looked up at him, her face pale, her eyes defiant. 'What does it matter if I am?'

Matter? He didn't deflower virgins. He didn't corrupt innocents. Having been heartbreakingly naive once himself, he had no desire to rip away the veil of innocence from someone else. Yet here he was, poised to do just that. If he was being completely honest with himself, he'd ignored every neon warning sign that had been flashing at him tonight, every obvious example of the evidence of her innocence and inexperience. Her total naivety.

'It matters,' he gritted out and, though it felt like the worst form of torture, he started to withdraw from her welcoming, silken entrance.

'No.' Lina hooked her legs around his hips, pulling him back inside her. Her expression was fierce, her eyes bright with determination. 'You can't ruin me without fulfilling your side of the bargain.'

He let out a choked laugh, every muscle straining as they engaged in this absurd, exquisite push and pull. 'My side of the bargain?'

'You said you were going to make love to me, Rico,' she stated fiercely. 'So do it.' And with that she wrapped her legs more tightly around his waist and pulled him deeper into her, wincing as she did so, but not hesitating for a second.

Rico muttered a curse as he sank deep inside her, his mind going hazy with the incredible feel of her body wrapped around his. His instinct was still to withdraw, to roll away from her and send her from the room. A *virgin*. A disaster.

Yet the tightly held shreds of his control were disintegrating under the welcoming heat of her body, and with a groan he surrendered to her, knowing she was the victor as their bodies began to move in that ancient, harmonious rhythm.

The least he could do for her was bring her back to that dazzling precipice, even as he climbed towards its heights. Rico watched in satisfaction as her face softened with pleasure, her eyes unfocused, pupils dilated, her breath coming out in a shuddery rush as her body convulsed around his. Then, and only then, did he find his own satisfaction, releasing himself inside her with a final groan of surrender.

For several moments afterwards his mind blurred and blanked as the last aftershocks of his climax pulsed through him. He rolled off her onto his back, one arm thrown over his eyes. Regret lanced him, a sword he threw himself on with bitterness—because he *knew* better. Of course he did.

He'd lost his self-control, he'd thrown it away with both hands, and for what? A single moment of pleasure? A damning *need*? He hated the thought. He didn't need anyone. He wouldn't let himself.

'Why,' he gritted out, his arm still over his eyes, 'did you come up to my hotel suite if you are— were—a virgin?'

She shifted next to him, pulling a sheet across her body. 'What does one thing have to do with the other?'

'You knew what I intended. I made it very clear, for a *reason*.'

'Yes.' She sounded calm and a little resigned, but not particularly regretful. Rico removed his arm from his eyes and turned to stare at her. Her face was rosy and flushed, her lips swollen, her eyes bright. She looked… She almost looked happy. He didn't understand it at all.

'Did you intend for this to happen?' he asked incredulously. 'Was that why you were waiting outside the party? Were you waiting for me?'

'Not for you in particular.'

His ego took a surprised bruising at that honest statement. 'So any man would have done?'

She bit her lip, her gaze sliding away from his. 'That sounds awful.'

'But that's what you're saying?' He felt outraged, even though he knew it was ridiculous. He'd had that very attitude countless times. He *preferred* that attitude…in himself. And one thing he was not was a hypocrite. Yet here he was, feeling offended by her honesty.

'No, that's not what I am saying.' Lina's eyes flashed and she scrambled up to a sitting position, her lush breasts on glorious display. She had the most amazing figure—curvy and womanly and round. Just looking at her made Rico ache all over again. Virgin or not, Lina still enflamed him.

She pulled the sheet up, wrapping it around herself as she glared at him, her chin tilted at a defiant angle. 'What does it matter to you?' she demanded. 'According to those women back in the bathroom, you should be showing me the door right about now.'

'Is that what you want?' Rico hurled back at her. He didn't even know why he was so angry, only that he was.

'It's what I *expected*. And wasn't that what this was all about? You warned me, Rico, about how little I could expect from you. Now it seems I'm getting more than I bargained for.' And she didn't sound very happy about it.

Rico stared at her in fury, wondering why he didn't just let her go. She was acting exactly the way he should want, but something compelled him to keep her here. He wanted answers. He also wanted her.

'It's different,' he ground out. 'Since you're a virgin.'

Lina rolled her eyes. 'That's my business, not yours.'

'You should have told me.'

'Why?'

'Because I never would have slept with you then!'

'And that's exactly why I didn't tell you.'

She was impossible. Rico rolled up to a sitting position and yanked on his trousers. A sudden thought occurred to him, terrible and profound. 'You said it

was safe.' From behind him Lina didn't say a word
and slowly Rico turned around. 'I asked you if you
were on birth control...'

Her eyes widened a fraction and she hitched the
sheet higher. 'That wasn't actually what you asked.'

'I asked if it was safe!'

'Which could mean something completely different.'

Cold dread swirled in his stomach, along with
an anger fiercer than he'd ever felt before. 'Most
women, when in the intimate situation we were in,
would know precisely what that meant.' He took a
deep breath and let it out slowly. 'Are you saying
you're not on birth control?' Why would she be, if she
was a virgin? Unless she'd taken it with the express
purpose of losing her virginity tonight. The thought
seemed so bizarre he didn't know what to do with it.
'Tell me you're on birth control.'

Lina shrugged, her ink-dark hair sliding about her
shoulders. 'Fine. I'm on birth control.'

'You're lying.'

'You asked me to tell you—'

Rico swore loudly and viciously. 'I didn't mean
for you to *lie*.' He raked a hand through his hair, his
fingers pulling on the short strands, frustration now
matching his fury and confusion. 'Lina, I don't understand you.'

'You don't need to.'

He knew she was right, and that infuriated him
all the more. He should just send her away. By this

point in an evening, usually he would already be in the shower, expecting his bed partner, whoever she was, to be finding her own way out. What was so different now?

'If you're not on birth control, you could be pregnant.' Lina lifted her chin another notch and said nothing. 'Damn it, Lina, that's a rather major issue, don't you think?'

A muscle flinched in her cheek. 'It's not your concern.'

'It is very much my concern,' Rico returned in a low, dangerous voice, certainty thrumming inside him. He would *never* abandon his own child, as he had once been abandoned. He would die first. 'If you are pregnant with my child, it is my paramount concern.'

Her face paled and she blinked slowly, seeming to absorb that statement. Rico shook his head, impatient as well as furious. 'Did it not even occur to you that you could become pregnant?'

'Not exactly.' She bit her lip. 'I wasn't thinking about that just then.'

'Then why on earth did you say it was safe? Did you lie on purpose?'

'I… I didn't understand what you meant.' Colour crept into her face and she looked away.

Rico stared at her incredulously. 'What did you think I meant, then?'

'I don't know.' Her voice rose in agitation. 'I wasn't thinking at all, to be honest.'

'Neither was I,' Rico returned grimly, hating that it was true. What a mess. And he had no one to blame but himself. He should have realised how naive she was. She'd given him plenty of clues.

Sitting in his bed, wrapped in his sheet, her hair everywhere, her eyes wide and her face pale, she looked very young and incredibly vulnerable. How could he have thought for a moment that she was experienced, a woman of the world? She was anything but.

'How old are you?' he asked abruptly and she gave him a look of scorn.

'Twenty-two, so you have no worries on that score.'

'Still—'

'I'm not your problem, Rico.'

'But you could be—' His words were cut off by a sudden buzzing. Lina looked at him questioningly.

'It's the lift,' he explained tersely. 'The doors lock automatically, since it opens right into the suite.' The buzzing sounded again, insistent. Whoever was in the lift wanted to get in. Who the hell was trying to find him now?

CHAPTER FOUR

HALINA WATCHED IN misery as Rico grabbed his shirt
and strode from the room. She slid from the bed, still
clutching the sheet to her, and reached for her dress.
She needed to get out of here as soon as possible,
before her mother or Abdul missed her. Before she
broke down completely and burst into tears in front
of Rico, appalling him even further.

How could she have been so *stupid*?

Hurriedly Halina snatched her underwear and
yanked it on before wriggling into her dress. She
managed to get the zip halfway up and decided that
would have to do. She couldn't find her bra, so she
just left it. She had to get out of here—now.

She needed to absorb everything that had happened tonight, everything she'd let happen, because
she'd been so befuddled, besotted and bewitched by
Rico Falcone. Those women had been right—he was
fabulous at sex.

Too bad that didn't do much for her now, when she
was facing a terrifyingly uncertain future. She looked
back on the last few hours, blurred as they were, and

marvelled that she'd been so reckless, with scarcely a thought for her future, her self. How could she have jeopardised everything for a single night's pleasure?

'What the hell are you doing?'

Halina's head jerked up at the sound of Rico's furious voice, and then her mouth dropped open in shock as the royal bodyguard, Abdul, strode into the bedroom. She'd thought things were bad enough but they'd just become a million times worse.

'Come now, Your Highness,' Abdul said in Arabic. He bowed his head so he didn't have to look upon her near-nakedness.

'Abdul…' Halina licked her lips, her mouth dry, her mind whirling. 'How did you…?'

'Please, Your Highness. Come now. Your mother is waiting.'

The balled tights she'd been clutching in one fist fell to the floor. 'Does my mother know…?' she began. Abdul's terse nod was all the confirmation she needed, and far more than she wanted. Any hope of creeping back into her hotel suite with no one the wiser crumbled to ash. Not only did she have to deal with the loss of her virginity and a possible pregnancy, but her parents' fury and disappointment. She swayed on her feet, sick with both fear and shame.

Rico stood in the doorway, looking furious. 'Who is this, Lina?' he demanded. His face was flushed, his shirt unbuttoned, his eyes blazing.

'I have to go,' Halina said numbly. She had to go now, before she passed out, or was sick, or burst into tears. She felt close to doing all three. With trembling fingers, she struggled with the rest of the zip. Rico muttered a curse and then crossed the room to her and did it up himself.

'Do not touch her again,' Abdul ordered in English, his voice flat and lethal, and Rico whirled on the man as if he'd been waiting for the chance to attack.

'*Excuse* me?'

'Please, Rico, just let me go.' Spots danced before her eyes and a pressure was building in her chest. She needed to get out of here *now*.

Rico glanced furiously at Abdul, who was waiting by the door, his arms crossed, his face studiously blank. 'Who is he? What is he to you?' he demanded.

'No one,' Halina answered quietly. 'No one like that. He's one of my guards.'

'*Guards?*'

'We must go now.' Abdul stepped forward, six-foot-four of solid muscle, but he paled in comparison with Rico in all his glittering fury, who looked as if he was seriously contemplating throwing a punch at the bodyguard.

'We aren't finished here, Lina,' Rico insisted in a voice that throbbed with angry intensity.

'We have to be,' Halina whispered, and she slipped by him towards the lift. As she stabbed the button she saw out of the corner of her eye Abdul block Rico's way. Rico looked mutinous, his fists clenched, his whole body taut with rage.

Thankfully the doors of the lift opened before he

did something precipitous, and Halina stepped inside with a shuddery sigh of both relief and regret, Abdul following quickly… The doors closed as Rico strode to face them, fury and disbelief etched on every rugged line of his face. Then she saw him no more.

All the courage and defiance Halina had felt earlier in the evening, all the excitement from being with Rico, had all gone, leaving her flattened and empty. She was terrified too, yet she knew she deserved everything she was going to get, which she couldn't bear to think about yet.

She glanced at Abdul, who was stony-faced and silent. 'How did you find me?' she whispered.

'It was not so difficult, Your Highness.'

'But how did you know I was gone?'

'I check all the rooms of the suite throughout the night.'

And she'd thought she was being so clever. She hadn't realised Abdul was so thorough, never mind that he'd dozed off for a few minutes.

He must have seen she was gone and then looked for her downstairs. The bouncer at the party could have identified her, as well as Rico, and how he'd seen them leave together. No, it had not been so difficult. And she was even more foolish than she'd realised.

'My mother…?' she began, but Abdul just shook his head. It was not his place to say what her mother thought.

Soon enough they were walking down the hallway to their hotel suite, and Halina's heart began to thud in an entirely new and unpleasant way at the prospect of facing her mother. What would Aliya Amar think of her daughter's flagrant disobedience? What would happen?

She didn't have to wait long to find out. As soon as Abdul swiped the key card, her mother threw open the door. She stood with her shoulders thrown back, her face flushed with both fury and fear, her eyes narrowed to dark slits.

'Leave us,' she commanded Abdul, and he did so.

Halina closed the door behind her, her fingers trembling on the knob. She'd never seen her mother look so angry. Her mother was always carefree and charming, her light laughter tinkling through the rooms of the royal palace of Abkar. Yet now she looked like a woman possessed by rage. Halina shrank back. She couldn't help it.

'I cannot believe you have been so stupid,' Aliya stated in a cold, restrained voice. 'So utterly reckless. We leave Abkar for one night—one night!—and you manage to completely disgrace yourself. How completely, I can see from the state of your dress.' She raked Halina with one up-and-down glance, taking in her rumpled dress, her lack of stockings, her tumbled hair and still-swollen lips. Halina felt as if the truth of her evening was written all over her, and she bowed her head.

'I'm sorry, Mama,' she whispered as tears gathered in her eyes. She couldn't even blame her mother for being so angry. She knew she deserved it, and more.

From the moment she'd escaped her bedroom she'd acted foolishly, without a thought to her future. Now that it was all over, she couldn't believe she'd been so completely stupid.

'I always knew you were impulsive,' Aliya continued. 'Ever since you were a little girl, going after whatever you fancied. Doing whatever you liked.'

'That's not fair!' Halina protested, even though she knew it was unwise to argue. She'd been spoiled a little, yes. She could acknowledge that. But her life had been so restricted, with so little opportunity for fun or excitement. Halina knew it didn't justify her actions, but at least it explained them a little.

'Fair?' Aliya repeated, her voice ringing out. 'You want to talk to me about fair?' She whirled away from Halina, pacing the sumptuous carpet of the suite's living area. Then she stopped, her back to Halina, her shoulders slumping. 'Heaven help us both, Halina,' she whispered. 'What am I going to tell your father? He is going to be devastated. Heartbroken. This affects everything. All our plans…the political alliances that are so important…'

Halina swallowed, blinking back more tears. She hated the thought of disappointing her father so badly. She didn't even understand why she'd done it. Had Rico Falcone really possessed that kind of hold on her? In the heat of the moment, he had. Even now she could recall a flicker of that intoxicating pleasure, the way it had blurred her mind and emboldened her actions.

Aliya turned slowly to face her. 'Who was this man? Why did you meet him? Was it planned?'

'I…' Halina stared at her helplessly. What answer could she give? 'It wasn't planned. I… I was scared,' she finally whispered.

'Scared? Did this man scare you?'

'No, not like that. I…' Her mind whirled. 'Olivia's kidnapping frightened me. It made me realise how little I've experienced, how little chance I've had to have fun…'

'Fun?' Her mother looked incredulous. 'This was about having *fun*?'

It made her sound so silly, so shallow, and in truth Halina knew she'd been both. 'I just wanted to go to a party,' she said. Aliya shook her head slowly. 'To see something of life, to feel…alive.'

'You are such a child, Halina. Do you have any idea what is at stake?'

'I never meant things to go so far.' Yet she'd chosen her fate. Halina knew she couldn't pretend otherwise. Rico had given her the opportunity to walk away and she hadn't taken it.

'How far did you go, Halina?' Aliya demanded in a low voice. 'As far as I fear, judging by the look of you?'

Halina said nothing. Her throat was too tight to speak. Her mother whirled around again, her fingers pressed to her temples.

'I cannot even believe…' she began in a throaty whisper. 'Could you be pregnant? Is that a possibility?'

'No.' The denial, the lie, was instinctive, and Halina desperately wanted to believe it. She *couldn't* be pregnant. She just couldn't. Aliya turned around slowly.

'Because if you were,' she said, 'we would have to get rid of it. I know how heartless that sounds, but as a royal family we cannot endure the scandal. It would shame us all, and ruin your sisters' potential matches.'

Halina kept her mother's gaze even as she quailed inwardly at Aliya's total ruthlessness. Get rid of her child? No matter how much she'd wrecked her future, Halina knew she would never want that. But she hated the thought that what she'd done might affect her three younger sisters, who were still in the schoolroom and even more innocent than she was— or, rather, had been.

'There's no chance,' she said firmly, willing herself to believe it along with her mother. Inside her everything shook. Her future felt more uncertain than ever. She had no idea what was going to happen to her now.

Rico stared at the hazy landscape of Rome's buildings in the muggy summer heat, unable to concentrate on the property deal laid out on his desk. All he needed to do was review a few simple terms and scrawl his signature. Yet his brain had stalled, as it had many times over the last two months, ever since Lina had left his hotel suite in a cloud of confusion and shame.

It hadn't been difficult to find out who she was—

Princess Halina of Abkar, known to be a spoiled pet of her father, a guest of the hotel where the party had been held and presently engaged to Prince Zayed al bin Nur of Kalidar. The fact that he'd deflowered a virgin promised to another man was like a stone in Rico's gut.

He might be considered cold and ruthless—he'd been called emotionless and even cruel—but he was a man of honour, and in lying to him Halina had made him violate his own personal code of morality. It was one he'd lived by staunchly since his days in the orphanage, determined to rise above the desperation and poverty, to be better than those around him, because that had felt like all he'd had. He didn't lie, steal or cheat. He never would. But in taking Halina to his bed he felt he'd done all three. It was something he could not forgive himself.

But, regardless of whether or not he could forgive her for lying to him, he needed to know where she was… and if she was pregnant. Because no matter what he felt for Halina he would take care of his child. His blood. That was a certainty. The very idea that he might be put in the position his mother had been in, a stranger to his own child, was anathema to him. His mother might not have cared about her own child, but he did. He would. Absolutely.

The day after Halina had left his suite Rico had hired a private investigator to discover where she was and what she was doing, determined to find her, and more importantly to discover if she was pregnant.

The possibility that she might be carrying his child and marry someone else burned inside him. He would never allow such a travesty; it would be even worse than her simply being pregnant. But as the days slipped by with no answer he knew he might have to; it might have already happened.

The thought of another man raising his child, passing him off as his own, made his fists clench and brought bile to the back of his throat. *Never.* But he'd had no word from the investigator who had flown to Abkar to ferret out information.

All he knew was that Halina had returned to Abkar the day after their encounter and hadn't been seen since, although she was believed to be residing in the royal palace. Attempts to get any information or gain entrance to the palace had been fruitless, so he had no idea if she'd married al bin Nur as planned or if she was pregnant.

Rico turned away from the window, pacing the confines of his luxurious office. For the last eight weeks he'd lived in a torment of ignorance and uncertainty, unable to focus on anything until he knew the outcome of his one night with Halina.

He'd told himself it was unlikely she was pregnant, that in all likelihood he'd never see her again and never needed to. His own history made that hope a faint one. His mother had been a waitress, his father a worker on Salerno's docks. They'd had one night together and he'd been the unwanted result. His mother had dumped him with his father when he'd been two weeks old and walked away, never to return. He'd been a mistake, a terrible inconvenience, and he'd never been able to forget it. He would not allow his own child to suffer a similar fate.

'Signor Falcone?' The crackle of his intercom had him turning. He reached over and pressed a button. 'Yes?'

'A Signor Andretti to see you, *signor*,' his assistant said, and Rico's heart leapt with fierce hope. Andretti was the private investigator he'd hired a month ago. 'Send him in.'

Moments later the neatly dressed man, slim and anonymous-looking, stepped into Rico's office.

'Well?' Rico demanded tersely. 'Is there news?'

'The marriage to al bin Nur has been called off. Apparently the Princess refused to marry him, and so he is remaining married to the governess he kidnapped.'

Rico had heard already, through the investigator, how Halina's fiancé had kidnapped the wrong woman and married her in so much haste that he hadn't ascertained her name first. A fool's mistake, one he would never make. He dismissed them both; they were irrelevant to him now that he knew Halina had called off the marriage. 'And the Princess?'

'I believe she is currently staying in a royal residence in the north of Abkar, a remote location.'

'Are you sure?'

Andretti shrugged. 'I bribed a maid in the palace, who told me the Princess had left about a month ago.

It seems the Princess is going to stay in the north for some time…' Andretti paused meaningfully. 'At least nine months.'

Nine months. Shock iced through him, followed by a fiery rage. She must be pregnant and she hadn't told him. Hadn't even tried to tell him. Instead she'd gone into hiding…*hiding from him?* He took a deep breath, steadying himself.

'Thank you.' As his head cleared a new emotion took the place of that first lick of anger, something that took him by surprise. Hope. Joy. If Halina was pregnant…he was going to be a father. He was going to have a child. One he would keep by his side, for whom he would fight to the death Someone he would never, ever leave. Not as he'd been left.

'Do you have the location of the palace?'

Andretti withdrew a folded piece of paper from his pocket. 'Right here, *signor.*'

It took Rico only a few hours to make the necessary arrangements. By nightfall he was on a plane to Abkar's capital city, where the following morning he picked up the all-terrain SUV he'd bought over the phone. The palace where Halina was staying was three hundred miles north of the city through inhospitable desert, a landscape of huge, craggy boulders and endless sand. She really must have wanted to get away from him.

Of course, she could have been banished there but, judging from all the gossip Rico had heard through the private investigator about how the Sultan spoiled his four daughters, Rico doubted it. This was a choice Halina had made. A decision to hide from him.

He drove the first hundred miles before the sun got too hot, his body taut with suppressed energy, his mind focused with grim purpose on the task ahead.

When the sun reached its zenith he stopped the Jeep and sheltered under a rock from the worst of the midday heat. Along with the SUV he'd arranged for provisions to survive in the desert for a week. He always made sure to be prepared in every situation, even one as extraordinary as this.

As for when he arrived at the palace... His mouth curved grimly. He would be prepared then, as well.

He stopped again for the night and then drove as soon as the first pearly-grey light of dawn lightened the sky. The sun had risen and bathed the desert in a fierce orange glow by the time he arrived at the palace, a remote outpost that looked as if it had been hewn from the boulders strewn about the undulating dunes.

Rico parked the SUV far enough away that he wouldn't be noticed and grabbed a pair of binoculars. From this distance the palace's walls looked smooth and windowless; the place truly was a fortress, and the nearest town of any description was over a hundred miles away. Halina had chosen as remote a place as possible to hide from him, but it was no place for a young pregnant woman. The sooner he got Halina out of there, the better.

As the mother of his child she belonged with

him—by his side, in his bed. As the mother of his child, she would raise that child with him, so he or she would never know a day without love, would never feel abandoned, an inconvenience to be discarded. A child needed both mother and father, and Halina would be there for their child and for Rico…as his wife.

CHAPTER FIVE

HALINA GAZED OUT of the window of her bedroom at the endless desert and suppressed a dispirited sigh. She'd been at Mansiyy Rimal, the Palace of Forgotten Sands, for nearly a month and it had been the longest month of her life. The prospect of spending several more months here filled her with despair, but it was better than contemplating what might come after that.

The week after her night with Rico was a blur of misery and fear. Her father, always so genial and cheerful, had become a complete stranger, cold and frightening in his fury, and Halina had shrunk before him, afraid of a man who had had only cause to spoil and indulge her until now.

He'd forced her to take a pregnancy test as soon as possible, and when it had come up positive the bottom had dropped out of Halina's stomach—and her world. She'd waited, barricaded in her bedroom, forbidden even to see her younger sisters, on whom she was now considered a bad influence, while her father negotiated on her behalf. He wanted her to marry Prince Zayed after all, now that she was spoiled goods and unsuitable for any other man. And Prince Zayed had seemed willing to go ahead, although reluctant.

Halina had used her last remnant of strength to resist such a fate, especially when she'd seen how Zayed and Olivia had fallen in love with each other. She'd thought she could bear a loveless marriage, but not when her husband so obviously cared for someone else.

Her steadfast refusal was the straw that had broken the remaining remnant of her father's terse goodwill. Halina still couldn't bear to think of the torturous aftermath, those days of despair and fear. Eventually, in cold fury, her father had sent her here to this remote outpost in the cruellest stretch of desert, with only a few stony-faced staff for company, to remain until she gave birth.

After that she had no idea what would happen to her or her child, and that was something that filled her with terror. The Sultan had warned her that he would take her child away from her, but Halina tried to believe that once his grandchild was born he would relent. Her father loved her. At least, he had once. Surely he couldn't be so cruel, despite how she'd disappointed him? Yet he'd already shown just how cruel he could be.

Escape was an impossibility—she was constantly watched by the palace staff, and in any case there was three hundred miles of inhospitable desert between her and the nearest civilisation. She was well and truly trapped.

Halina turned from the window, surveying the spartan room that was to be her bedchamber for the coming months. The palace was a barren place both inside and out, without any modern conveniences or amusements. All she had were a few books, some drawing materials and endless time.

Halina pressed one hand to her still-flat stomach, trying to fight the nausea that had become her constant companion a few weeks ago. She felt lonelier than she'd ever imagined feeling, and far more grown up. She looked back on her evening with Rico and wanted to take her old, girlish self by the shoulders and give her a hard shake. What on earth had she been thinking? Why had she gambled her future away for a single, reckless encounter? The sex, fabulous as it had felt at the time, most certainly had not been worth it.

Restlessly Halina plucked a sketchbook from the table and a few charcoal pencils. She'd always enjoyed sketching, and now she had endless hours to hone her skill. Not that there was much to draw but craggy rocks and sand dunes.

A sudden commotion from outside her room had Halina stilling, the charcoal barely touched to the paper.

'You cannot, sir!' Ammar, one of the palace staff, exclaimed, then the door was thrown open so hard it rocked on its hinges, swinging back and hitting the wall.

Rico Falcone stood there, dressed in desert camouflage fatigues, his sharp cheekbones flushed, his eyes glittering. Halina's mouth dropped open and she found she couldn't speak.

'You,' he said in a low, authoritative voice, 'Are coming with me.'

Ammar burst in behind him. 'You cannot take the Princess!'

'The Princess is pregnant with my child,' Rico returned evenly, the words vibrating with taut anger. 'She is coming with me.' His tone left no room for disagreement.

For a second Ammar looked uncertain. He wasn't trained to defend the palace; it was remote, as forgotten as its name, and he was nothing more than a steward, meant to fetch and carry. Sultan Hassan had never anticipated anyone looking for Halina, much less finding her. She was here with a skeleton staff who were more used to cooking and gardening than wielding arms or defending the ancient stone walls.

'Halina.' Rico stretched out one hand. 'Come now.'

Halina would have resented his commanding tone if she'd felt she had any choice. But when the alternative to going with Rico was mouldering in this palace, and then in all likelihood having her baby taken away from her, she knew what she'd choose. What she had to choose. Wordlessly she rose from where she sat and crossed the room to take his hand.

The feel of his warm, dry palm encasing hers sent a shower of untimely sparks through Halina's arm and then her whole body. Quite suddenly, and with overwhelming force, she remembered just how much she'd been attracted to Rico. How he'd overpowered her senses, her reason, everything. And how completely dangerous that had been.

He pulled her towards him and then started down the steep, turreted stairs while Ammar made useless noises of protest.

'Wait—what about my things?'

'I will buy you whatever you need.'

A shiver of apprehension rippled over her skin. What exactly was she agreeing to?

'What am I to tell the Sultan?' Ammar demanded, sounding both furious and wretched.

Rico turned, his hand still encasing hers. 'You may tell the Sultan,' he said in a low, sure voice, 'That Princess Halina is with the father of her child, where she belongs, and where she will stay.'

Ammar's mouth opened silently and Halina had no time to ask questions or reconsider her choice as Rico led her out of the palace with sure, confident strides.

'How on earth did you get here?' she demanded as he strode through the courtyard and then out the front gates.

'I bought an SUV.'

'And how did you get Ammar to open the gates?'

'I told him who I was.'

'You mean—?'

'A billionaire with considerable power and the father of your child.' He turned back to subject her to a dark glance. 'He saw reason quite quickly. Why did you not tell me, Halina?'

'Not *tell* you?' Halina repeated in disbelief. 'As if—'

He cut her off with a slash of his hand. 'Now is not the time. We need to get back to Rome.'

'Rome,' Halina repeated faintly. 'You're taking me to *Rome*?'

Rico gave her another scathing look. 'Of course. Where else would we go?'

'I… I don't know.' She felt dizzy with everything that had happened so quickly. She didn't even know what questions to ask, what answers she was ready to hear. Why had Rico taken her? What was he going to do with her?

They'd reached Rico's SUV parked a short distance from the palace behind a cluster of craggy rocks.

'You know,' Halina said shakily as Rico opened the passenger door and she climbed in, 'Ammar will radio my father and he'll send out guards to find us. To take me back.' Her father would be furious that after everything she'd been kidnapped after all. And Halina knew he wouldn't leave her alone once her baby was born. He'd take away her child and then marry her to whomever he could find that was politically suitable and willing to take damaged goods.

'I am not worried about your father,' Rico dismissed.

'Maybe you should be,' Halina tossed back. She couldn't believe she'd forgotten how impossibly arrogant he was. 'Considering he is a head of state and he will send out trained soldiers who know this terrain far better than you do.'

'True, which is why I will not be traversing it,' Rico informed her shortly. He swung into the driver's side and then pulled away, choking clouds of sand and dust rising as the tyres peeled through the desert. Halina pressed back against the seat, every movement jolting right through her bones.

'Where are we going, then?'

'North, to Kalidar. I have a helicopter waiting at the border.'

'A helicopter?' Halina stared at him in disbelief. 'How did you arrange such a thing? How did you even find me?'

'I told you that if you were pregnant you would be my paramount concern.'

'Yes, but...' Halina shook her head slowly. Rico's steadfast determination shocked, humbled and terrified her all at once. What else was this man, this stranger, capable of? The father of her child. 'Where will we go after Kalidar?' she asked numbly.

'I told you, Rome. I have a private jet waiting to take us there in its capital city, Arjah.' Rico's face was set in grim lines as he navigated the rocky terrain. 'We should be at the helicopter within the hour.'

Halina lapsed into silence, still dazed by the day's events. To think only moments ago she'd been contemplating how bored she would be, stuck in a desert palace for the better part of a year. Now she didn't know what to feel.

The jolting movements of the SUV eventually lulled her into an uneasy doze, only to wake when it stopped as Rico cut the engine. The sun was hot and bright above, creating a dazzling sparkle on the undulating sand dunes. In front of them was a helicopter bearing Kalidar's military insignia.

'How...?' Halina began, but then merely shook her head. Should she really be surprised at the extent of Rico's power? He was a billionaire, ruthless, arrogant and used to being obeyed. She had no doubt that he could get whatever he wanted...including her.

Rico helped her climb into the helicopter and then settled into a seat, putting on her headgear to muffle the powerful sound of the machine's blades as it started up into the sky.

Halina watched the desert drop away with fascinated disbelief, part of her still blessedly numb as she wondered what on earth her future held now—and how afraid she should be.

Rico stared straight ahead as the helicopter moved over the harsh and rugged landscape, a mixture of exultation and anger rushing through him. He'd done it. He'd found Halina. He'd brought her with him. Yet despite the triumph he felt at having accomplished that he couldn't let go of his anger that she would have hidden her pregnancy from him, his own child. Considering the nature of his origins and childhood, the possibility was even more repugnant to him. She would have turned him into a liar, the worst sort of man, without him even knowing.

He glanced at Halina who was sitting still, her hands

in her lap, her gaze resting on the horizon yet seeming to be turned inward. Her face was pale, her figure slenderer than when he'd last seen her. In fact, now that he was looking at her properly, she seemed entirely different from the innocent yet knowing siren who had tempted him in Rome wearing a sexy dress and stiletto heels, everything about her lush and wanton.

Now she was wearing a drab tunic and loose trousers in a nondescript beige, both garments hanging on her gaunt frame. Her hair, once loose and wild, was now secured in a simple ponytail low down on her neck. She was as far a cry from the woman he'd made love to as was possible. But despite what she'd done Rico felt an inconvenient shaft of desire as he remembered the feel of her body against his, the silken slide of her limbs and the honeyed sweetness of her mouth. He looked away, determined not to give in to that unwanted emotion right now.

The next time he slept with Halina, it would be as her husband, their relationship made permanent for the sake of their child and the security he intended his son or daughter to know. The next time he slept with Halina, he wouldn't lose control. Even now the memory of how far he'd gone, how lost in her he'd been, made him grit his teeth with regret and shame. Never again.

The helicopter started to descend, and moments later they touched down in a remote and barren location where he'd arranged for another SUV to pick them up and take them to Arjah, from where they would fly to Rome.

Halina looked startled as she gazed around at the landscape, as inhospitable as at the Palace of Forgotten Sands.

'Where are we?' she asked as she took Rico's proffered hand and stepped out of the helicopter. The wind was kicking up, blowing sand everywhere, and she lifted one slender hand to shield her eyes from the dust.

'We're about a hundred miles from Arjah.'

Her eyes widened. 'So far?'

'Such measures were necessary.' He hadn't been sure how Sultan Hassan would respond, and he wanted to deal with the head of state on his own terms, back in Italy with Halina as his wife, not during some ill-advised skirmish in the desert.

Halina's lips trembled and she pressed them together. 'I see.' Her face was pale, and she swayed slightly where she stood. Rico realised, with an uncomfortable jolt, that she was tired. Exhausted, by the looks of it. And, of course, pregnant.

'Not too much longer now,' Rico said, even though it would be another three or four hours at least jolting across the desert in the SUV until they reached Arjah.

'Okay,' Halina murmured, and headed towards the car. She fell asleep curled up on the back seat, her dark hair spread over the seat. Rico had dismissed the driver, who had joined the helicopter pilot in a safe return to Abkar. It was just the two of them as the night fell, stars twinkling in an endless sky, until the wind started up again and obliterated nearly everything.

After another hour of painstakingly inching across the rugged sands Rico was forced to stop. He glanced back at Halina, who had risen sleepily as she'd felt the vehicle come to a halt.

'Are we there…?'

'No.' Rico's voice was terse. This wasn't part of his plan. This was out of his control, and he didn't like it. 'It looks like a sandstorm is brewing.' He'd known it was a possibility, but he'd hoped they could afford being caught in the crosswinds. 'We'll have to spend the night here.'

'Here? Where?' Halina pushed her hair out of her face as she looked around. There was nothing to see but dust and dark. 'But…where are we?'

'In the middle of nowhere,' Rico said with a humourless laugh. 'About fifty miles from Arjah.' Spending the night in the middle of a sandstorm was not a good idea, but he didn't have any others. It was too dangerous to keep driving.

'But it's a sandstorm,' Halina said, and she sounded genuinely afraid. 'Rico, do you know how dangerous these are? People can be swallowed up in an instant—*consumed!*'

'I know.' Grimly he reached for a kerchief and tied it around his nose and mouth. 'Stay in the car and cover your face when I open the door.'

'What are you doing?'

'Going out to make us a shelter.'

'But shouldn't we stay in the car?'

'No, because it will be buried by the sand, and then we'll never get out.'

'Oh.' She swallowed, her fragile throat working, her face pale, eyes wide. 'All right.' Setting her chin with a determined courage that strangely touched Rico's hardened heart, she lifted her tunic to cover her mouth and nose.

Taking a deep breath, Rico opened the door. The wind and sand hit him full in the face, making his eyes sting and cutting off his vision. Despite the covering of his mouth and nose, the sand worked its way in, filling his mouth with grit and choking him.

Quickly Rico closed the door behind him and hunched his shoulders against the unforgiving onslaught. He gathered provisions from the back of the SUV—a tent, water, food and blankets. As swiftly as he could, his head bowed against the relentless wind and sand, he erected a tent against the partial shelter of a massive boulder. It wasn't much, but it would help a little against the wildness of the wind and sand.

Then he battled his way back to the car which was already becoming covered in sand and grit. He wrenched open the door and reached for Halina; she grabbed onto his hand with both of hers.

With his arm around her shoulders, their heads tucked low, he led her to their shelter, pulling the flap closed behind them and taping it shut to keep out the blowing sands.

Halina fell onto the floor of the tent on her hands and knees, coughing.

'Are you all right?' Rico knelt next to her, one hand on her back as she shuddered and coughed.

'Yes,' she finally gasped out. "Although I feel as if I've swallowed half of the Sahara.' She looked up blinking, her hair tangled about her sand-dusted face.

'Here.' He reached for one of the plastic gallon containers of water he'd arranged to have packed in the SUV. Fortunately they would not suffer through the storm, as long as they could stay safe through the worst of the wind.

Rico poured a tin cup full of water and handed it to her. 'Slowly,' he advised, and she nodded and took a few careful sips. He held her gaze as she drank; he'd forgotten how lovely and dark her eyes were, how thick and full her lashes. Something stirred inside him, something half-forgotten and ever-insistent.

'Thank you,' she murmured as she lowered the cup. Rico dabbed the corner of a cloth in the remaining water and then gently wiped the sand from her face. Halina sucked in a shocked breath, staying completely still as he swept the cloth along her forehead and cheekbones, her dark, wide gaze tracking his.

What he'd intended to be expedient and practical suddenly felt erotic and charged. Desire throbbed through him as he continued to wipe the sand away, conscious of Halina's soft skin beneath his fingers, the pulse hammering in her throat, every hitched breath she drew.

'Rico…' His name was a whisper, whether plea or protest he didn't know. He dropped the cloth, not wanting the distraction of desire at this point, as insistent as it was. He needed to focus on their future… their child.

'You should eat,' he said roughly. 'You need to keep up your strength. You look as if you have wasted away to little more than skin and bone.'

'I've had morning sickness. All day sickness, really.' She smiled wanly but her eyes were dark and troubled. 'You're angry. Why?'

He was, but he disliked how she made this about his unruly emotion rather than her deliberate actions. 'Eat,' he said as he yanked out some pita bread and dried meat. 'Then we'll talk.'

Halina took the bread and nibbled on it, barely swallowing a mouthful. 'What are we going to talk about?'

'We could begin,' Rico said, an edge entering his voice, 'with why you dared to attempt to hide your pregnancy from me. Going all the way to that god-forsaken place to keep it from me, even.' His eyes flashed fire and the pita bread dropped from Halina's fingers.

'Is that what you think…?'

'It's what I know.' He picked up the bread and pushed it towards her. 'But first, eat. There will be time enough to discuss the past…as well as our future.'

CHAPTER SIX

HALINA STARED AT Rico in disbelief, although why she should be surprised by his high-handed manner she had no idea. It was par for the course. Still, she struggled to find a suitable reply. Her mind was spinning and her stomach seethed. She was not at her best for an all-out confrontation.

'Eat,' Rico said again, and because she knew she needed the sustenance, she nibbled the pita once more. 'You look terrible,' he remarked after a moment and she let out a huff of humourless laughter.

'Why, thank you very much.'

'Why have you not been taking care of yourself?'

She lowered the bit of bread and eyed him with disbelief. 'Seriously? You're going to ask me that?'

'What else am I supposed to ask?'

She shook her head. 'God only knows. You blame me for everything, even being a virgin.'

'You should have told me.'

'Not that again. Are we going to revisit that particular argument now?'

'No,' Rico answered tightly. 'We are not.'

Which made Halina's stomach clench unpleasantly because she didn't think she wanted to talk about the other matters that might be on Rico's agenda. The courage that had been buoying her briefly, sparked by his sheer pig-headedness, trickled away.

She glanced at him from under her lashes, taking in the obdurate set of his jaw, the sharp cheekbones, the hard eyes. She'd forgotten how intimidating he was, especially when he wasn't trying to get her into bed.

The memory of just how easily she'd tumbled into that bed made her cringe with shame. She'd had nearly two months of public and private shame to deal with—her father's icy fury, her mother's heart-broken disappointment, her own inner torment. Even the lowliest of the palace staff had sensed her humili-ation. No one had remained unscathed by her actions, least of all herself. When she thought of what she'd almost had to do…

She tossed the bread aside, her stomach too un-settled even to think of food. Rico frowned.

'I said you should eat.'

'I know, but I don't feel up to it. And I don't think you want me retching in this small space.' She wrapped her arms around her knees, feeling lonelier even than she had when she'd been at the Palace of Forgotten Sands, and the days had been endless and empty. Now she was in a tiny, enclosed space with a man who seemed to be taking up all the air and en-ergy and she felt even more alone…and afraid. The relief that she'd been rescued was replaced by a greater fear. 'Frying pan and fire' came alarmingly to mind.

'Try the meat,' Rico said gruffly, handing her a strip of meat that looked as tough as leather. Halina couldn't tell if he was trying to be kind or just insistent. She took it reluctantly, because she really was feeling wobbly inside. Even though she didn't like Rico's methods or manner, she knew he was right. She'd lost nearly a stone since the nausea had hit. For her baby's sake, she needed to eat.

'Has your morning sickness been very bad?' he asked after a moment as she worried the salted meat with her teeth.

'Yes.' Halina swallowed. 'For the last month or so I've barely been able to keep anything down.' She managed a wry smile, her tone tart. 'Which is why I look so terrible.'

Rico, of course, did not look remotely abashed by her reminder. 'You need to take better care of yourself. Why hasn't your doctor prescribed something for the nausea?'

Halina stared at him, torn between fury and an exhausted exasperation. 'I haven't seen a doctor.' Not one she wanted to remember, anyway. The one doctor she'd seen… But, no. She didn't want to think about that.

'What?' Rico's mouth dropped open in outrage before he snapped it shut, his eyes narrowing. 'Why on earth not?'

She shook her head wearily. 'You have no idea.'

'Then enlighten me.'

Halina sat back, wondering whether she had the strength or will to explain to Rico about the last two months, and then no doubt be subjected to his scorn and condemnation—or maybe just his disbelief.

'Lina.' His voice was rough, urgent. '*Ha*lina. Tell me what you mean.'

'I was called Lina as a child,' she said inconsequentially. 'I didn't lie when I told you that's what my name was.'

'That is hardly my concern now.'

'But it was before.' She was splitting hairs, but she was too emotionally fragile to battle all this out now. 'Rico, I'm tired and it's raging out there. Can't we leave this for a little while?' Maybe another day she'd have the strength to admit everything she'd endured. As for now, she just wanted to sleep, if she could.

The wind had picked up even more and was battering the sides of the tent, howling around them, a relentless monster eager for prey.

Rico gave a terse nod. 'Very well. As you say, now is not the time or the place—but I will have answers, Halina. Of that there is no doubt.'

'Fine.'

He unrolled two sleeping bags and shook them out. With an entirely different kind of queasy feeling, Halina realised how close they'd be sleeping to each other—shoulder to shoulder, thigh to thigh. Not that anything was going to happen in the middle of a sandstorm, and with her feeling like a plate of left-over pudding. But still… She was aware of him. Even now.

She adjusted the shapeless tunic and trousers she wore, as if they could offer her more coverage. As if Rico would even be tempted. She knew she looked terrible and he'd already told her so. Feeling silly for even considering such a possibility, Halina scooted into the sleeping bag and drew it up to her chin.

Rico eyed her for a moment, his mouth compressed, a look of cool amusement on his features.

'Are you worried for your virtue?' he drawled. 'Because, I assure you, it's not in any danger.'

'I don't have any virtue left to lose,' Halina retorted. 'You made sure of that.'

Rico's face darkened. 'Are you going to blame me for that now? Because—'

'No, Rico, I'm not. I should have told you. Trust me, I know. I wish I had, because then—' She cut off that unfortunate thought before she could give it voice. She would not regret her baby. It had already cost her too much, innocent life that it was. 'I just want to go to sleep,' she said. And then, pointedly, she turned away from him on her side and closed her eyes.

Sleep, however, felt impossible. Her stomach seethed, as did her mind. What was she doing here? And what was going to happen? Her life was in chaos, and the only sure thing was the baby nestled in her womb. But even that little one's life was being thrown up in the air like a set of dice… Rico was entirely in control, as he always was. Whether she was in a fortress or a tent, Halina acknowledged starkly, she was still imprisoned, her fate at the whim of another, and in this case a complete stranger.

Next to her she heard Rico moving around and then sliding into his sleeping bag. The rustle of fabric in the darkness felt intimate, and Halina inched a little bit away, not that there was much room.

Inconvenient memories were sliding through her mind in an all too vivid montage. The feel of Rico's body on hers. In hers. The way she'd given herself to him, utterly and overwhelmingly. It had felt as if she hadn't even had a choice, but of course she had. She'd just made the wrong one.

Then, even though it only hurt, Halina let herself think that treacherous *what if?* What if she hadn't been so stupid as to sacrifice her entire future for a single night with Rico Falcone? Where would she be now? Would Zayed al bin Nur have stayed married to her friend Olivia? Halina hoped so. She knew they were in love, and it would have been even worse to be married to a man who loved another than to be where she was now, pregnant and shackled to a man who regarded her with contempt and disdain.

So if Zayed stayed married to Olivia and she hadn't been pregnant…right now she might be free, the future stretched out in front of her, shining and brimming with possibility.

Of course, realistically her father would have arranged another marriage to another suitable stranger, but Halina didn't want to think about that now. She had enough to deal with, sleeping next to *this* unsuitable stranger.

'Stop wriggling around,' Rico said irritably, his voice sounding loud in the enclosed space.

'I'm not wriggling,' Halina returned indignantly. 'I'm barely moving.' She'd been staying completely still, as if Rico might forget she was there.

Rico just sighed as if she were simply too tedious to deal with. It was going to be a long night. It was going to be a long life. What had Rico meant, 'their future'? She shuddered to think.

Eventually, simply because she was so utterly exhausted, Halina fell into a restless doze, only to wake suddenly, her body on high alert.

'What…?' she began, blinking in the darkness. Outside the wind was shrieking, and the sides of the tent sagged inwards from the weight of both the wind and the sand, and Halina felt as if she was being entombed. Perhaps she was.

A shudder of terror went through her and she whimpered out loud. The storm raged all around them, seemingly ready to consume their tent in its ravenous maw. Heaven help them both, was this going to be the end of them both?

'It will pass.' Rico's voice was low and steady, a thrum of comfort.

'How do you know?' Halina asked in a high, faltering voice. 'We could be buried alive.' She started to tremble, her teeth chattering with pure, unadulterated fear.

Then, to her shock, she felt Rico's hands on her shoulders and he pulled her against him, fitting her body next to his so she could feel the hard, warm press of his chest, his powerful thighs.

She stayed rigid with shock for a few seconds, then Rico began to rub comforting circles over her back with the palm of his hand, and Halina started to relax.

It felt so good to be held. It felt so safe. Until this moment she hadn't realised how much she craved both the comfort and security of another person's touch. She closed her eyes as she snuggled into him, telling herself this didn't count. Extraordinary measures for extraordinary circumstances—that was all this was. In the morning she would be back to keeping her distance and composure—and regaining her strength.

Rico continued to rub Halina's back as he felt her melt into him and he tried not to react. Even in her gaunt state she was pliant, warm and womanly. He desired her even now, with the storm raging all around them and their lives at stake.

'Have you never been in a sandstorm before?' he asked, trying to distract himself from his own demanding need.

'No, I've only seen them from a distance. From the safety of a palace.' She let out a choked laugh, her breathing fanning his neck. 'I've led a very restricted life, Rico.'

A very privileged life. Her upbringing was a world

away from his on the docks of Salerno, a mother who hadn't wanted him at all and a father...

But why the hell was he thinking about his father now?

Seeing Halina, knowing she was carrying his child, had opened a need in him and, worse, a vulnerability that he struggled to contain. Control was paramount. He would provide for his child, he would love him or her, his own flesh and blood, he would make a stable family that his child could trust in absolutely. But he would not give in to this inconvenient and shaming need; he would never allow himself to be weak.

To make the point to himself, he inched a little bit away from Halina's soft, tempting body. Outside the wind howled and the tent continued to be battered mercilessly.

'Have you ever been in a sandstorm?' Halina asked, moving closer to him again, one fine-boned hand resting on his chest. Resigned, Rico put his arms more securely around her, telling himself he was doing it for her sake, not his own.

'No, I have not.'

'Then you don't know if it will pass.'

'I checked the weather before I set out on this journey. The high winds were only meant to last a few hours.'

'Somehow I don't think sandstorms bow down to weather reports,' Halina returned. 'They are entirely unpredictable, coming out of nowhere, sometimes lasting for days.' Her voice hitched. 'What if we're stuck out here for that long? What if we're buried alive?'

'We won't be.'

'You don't know that, Rico. You don't control nature, as much as you might like to.'

Of course he didn't, but he prided himself on living a life where he always maintained control. Where he was always totally prepared. Where nothing ever surprised him, because then he wouldn't betray himself, his doubt or his need. Yet, just as Halina had said, he could not control a sandstorm, and he feared this was just the beginning of all the things he would not be able to control.

His arms tightened around Halina. 'I admit, the storm is stronger than I anticipated, but I brought the necessary equipment and food, and we are well positioned to wait it out. We'll be safe, Halina. I will make sure of it.'

Halina relaxed a fraction. 'I'm sorry,' she murmured. 'I don't mean to overreact.'

Rico couldn't keep a wry smile from touching his lips as he stroked her hair. No matter his promises, they were in a life-threatening situation. He'd hardly call it overreacting. 'You're forgiven,' he said, and Halina let out a little huff of laughter.

'Even when you're being kind, you're arrogant, do you know that?'

'It isn't arrogance when I'm right.'

She just laughed again, her lips brushing his neck,

sending gooseflesh rippling along his skin. Desire arrowed through his body and he knew Halina felt it too by the way she tensed in his arms, shifting a little so she was looking up at him, her hair cascading down her back in an inky blue-black river that Rico could just make out in the darkness of the tent.

His mind blurred and he started to lower his head to claim her mouth with his own. He could imagine the kiss, the rightness of it. He could already taste it, like a drink of clean, sweet water. He heard Halina's quick, indrawn breath as she waited for him to close the space between their mouths and it shocked him into clarity. He lifted his head.

He could not complicate their relationship with sex. Not yet. Not until he'd made it very clear what he expected of Halina and their marriage. Of their life together, or lack of it. Until then, he'd keep his distance, for both their sakes.

He heard Halina draw another shuddering breath and knew she'd felt his withdrawal. She moved a little bit away from him, or tried to. Rico stilled her, keeping her close, although he wasn't sure why. Surely it was better to let her go, give them both a little distance? Still, he stayed where he was, and made sure she did as well.

'Go to sleep,' he said gruffly. Halina did not reply, but after a few endless moments he felt her body start to relax again, and then he heard the deep, even breaths of sleep as the storm continued to rage.

When he awoke the tent was hot and airless, awash

in a greyish morning light, and the world was still. Halina was still snuggled in his arms and now he could see her properly—the luxurious spill of her hair, her lush lips slightly parted, her thick, spiky lashes fanning onto her cheeks.

He brushed a tendril of hair from her face and her eyes fluttered open. For a taut second they simply stared at one another, their bodies pressed close together, Rico's already responding.

Halina moved away first, wriggling away from him as her face turned fiery. 'The storm has stopped,' she muttered as she scooted across the tent, putting as much space between them as she could, considering the limitations of their environment.

'So it has.'

She peered out, as if she could see right through the dark canvas. 'Are we going to be able to get out?'

'I should think so.'

It took some doing, but after Rico had torn the tape from the entrance to the tent he managed to dig them out.

'Only half-buried,' he said with a smile, and then reached for Halina's hand to help her out.

Outside they both stretched and blinked in the glare of the morning sunlight, the landscape made even more strange by the ravages of the storm. Drifts of sand were piled on either side of the tent and the SUV was completely buried, no more than a large hump in the sand. New dunes had formed, turning the once-flat stretch into a newly undulating lunar-like landscape.

'Goodness,' Halina murmured. Her arms were wrapped around herself, her face pale as she looked around. 'I'm amazed we're still here.'

'Yes.' Rico eyed the buried SUV. It would take him several hours to dig it out. 'We need to get going. Why don't you refresh yourself? Eat and drink something? I'll start digging out the car.'

'Why are we going to Rome, Rico?'

'Because that is where both my business and home are.' He rolled up his sleeves and started scooping the sand away from the car with his hands. Unfortunately he had not thought to pack a spade in his desert provisions.

'And what will we do when we get to Rome?' Halina pressed. Rico gritted his teeth. He didn't want to have this conversation, not until they were safely back in Rome, in his domain. But Halina seemed determined to discover his intentions, and Rico decided she might as well know them. It wasn't as if she could escape, anyway.

'We're going to Rome,' he said clearly, his gaze on the sand-covered car, 'because that is where we are going to live. Where my child is going to be born… and where you are going to marry me.'

CHAPTER SEVEN

HALINA STARED AT Rico in dawning realisation—and horror.

'Marry you?' she squeaked. *'That's* what you have in mind?'

'Yes.'

'But…but we don't know each other! And we don't even like each other.'

'I believe those statements are contradictory. And, in any case, you were prepared to marry more of a stranger to you than I am mere weeks ago.'

Halina flushed, not needing the reminder. 'I was prepared to do that out of duty,' she began, but fell silent when Rico gave a decisive shake of his head.

'And you will marry me out of duty as well. Duty to our unborn child.'

'We don't have to be married for our—'

'Yes.' Rico cut her off. 'We do. It is important to me, of paramount importance, that my child grows up in a stable and loving home.'

'Loving?' Halina repeated incredulously. 'But you don't love me.'

'I will love my child,' Rico stated flatly, his voice thrumming with certainly. 'But now is not the time to discuss this. We have more important matters to attend to.' He nodded towards the tent. 'Eat, drink and refresh yourself. We leave in an hour.'

Biting her lip, preferring not to argue with him when he was in such an intractable mood, Halina wordlessly turned and went back into the tent.

She choked down some more pita bread and dried meat, knowing she needed the sustenance, then washed her face with a sparing amount of water and rinsed out her mouth. With her hair tidied and her clothes straightened, she was as presentable as she was going to be, but she didn't feel at all ready for whatever lay ahead.

Marriage. She shouldn't have been surprised, she realised. Rico moved people about like pawns on his personal chessboard. Why should she, why should marriage, be any different?

Because he was the classic commitment-phobe who never kept a woman for more than a night. But with a sinking sensation Halina acknowledged that marriage to Rico Falcone was most likely not going to look or feel like a normal marriage. Not that she knew what that felt like. If she married Rico, she would just be exchanging one expedient union for another. One stranger for another. A loving, normal marriage had never been within her grasp, no matter how much she might have wanted it. Her life had never been her own.

Halina rolled up the sleeping bags and repacked their provisions in the canvas rucksack Rico had brought. Then, taking a deep breath, she went in search of her rescuer and captor.

He was hard at work digging out the SUV; he had shucked off his shirt and his tawny skin gleamed like polished bronze under the unforgiving glare of the desert sun. Halina blinked, trying not to let her gaze move slowly over his perfectly sculpted pectoral muscles, the six-pack definition of his taut abdomen. She failed and, even worse, Rico turned and caught her staring openly at his incredible physique.

His mouth quirked and something like satisfaction flashed in his eyes. He jerked his head in a nod towards their vehicle. 'I should be finished in another half hour.'

'Can I help…?'

'No, of course not. You're pregnant.'

'Pregnant, not an invalid.'

'Even so.' Rico turned back to the car. 'I do not wish you to tax yourself.'

With a sigh Halina wondered if Rico intended to wrap her in cotton wool for the next seven months. Then, with a jolt, she wondered why she was thinking this way. Was she just going to roll over and do whatever he said, including binding her life to his for ever? Would Rico let her do anything else?

Her choices, as ever, were limited. She'd never known what freedom felt like save, perhaps, for her one night with Rico. And look what had happened then.

Her mind in a ferment of indecision and uncertainty, Halina turned back to the tent. 'I'll pack up our things.'

Half an hour later the vehicle was clear and Rico had thrown their things into the back. His expression was grim and determined as he slid into the driver's seat. 'We have another two hours' drive to Arjah.'

'What if my father's soldiers are there? What if we're found?'

'We won't be.'

And if they were? Her father must have discovered her absence by now and most likely would have sent soldiers out to find her. And what then? Rico wouldn't give her up without a fight, but even he was no match against trained soldiers and weapons. Halina leaned her head back against the seat and closed her eyes. It was too much to think about on top of everything else.

'Any soldiers your father sent out would have been caught in the sandstorm, the same as we were,' Rico said. 'We have some time.'

Halina just nodded, not trusting herself to speak. In such a scenario she didn't even know what she'd prefer. To stay with Rico, or be rescued by her father? Both options seemed abysmal in their own way.

A bumpy few hours passed as they jolted along, the rough desert track gradually becoming a tarmac road, and then the low mud-brick buildings and handful of skyscrapers came into view—Arjah, the capital city of Kalidar.

Halina felt herself getting more and more tense as Rico drove through the city, his expression harsh and grim, his fingers tight on the steering wheel. They made it to the airport without notice, and Rico drove directly to a private plane waiting in its own bay.

Halina's breath came out in a shudder of relief that they had not been caught or detained. So she would prefer to stay with Rico. Her own reaction had betrayed her. That was why she'd left with him in the first place, she supposed—because she'd rather risk her future with this man than face the continuing wrath of her father, her baby taken away, her body given to a man she'd never even met.

Rico gave a grimly satisfied nod. 'It is just as I had arranged.' He parked the SUV and strode out to meet the plane's crew who were waiting for them on the tarmac. Halina followed, feeling exhausted and emotionally overwhelmed. If she got on that plane, it would take her all the way to Rome. And then where would she be? What would she do? What would Rico do?

'Come. There is no time to delay.' Rico beckoned her forward. 'You will be more comfortable on the plane.'

Halina hesitated, even though she knew there was no point. No choice. What was she going to do? Make a sprint for the airport? She had no money, no clothes, nothing. No resources at all, and no friends to help. For a second she thought of Olivia and Prince Zayed, who might be currently residing in the royal palace at

Arjah. She could seek sanctuary with them perhaps, but did she want to do that—be the unexpected and undoubtedly unwelcome guest of her former fiancé and his new bride? She'd be putting them into an impossible position as well as herself, and that was assuming she could even get to the royal palace from here, which she probably couldn't.

'Halina.' Rico's voice was touched with impatience. 'Everyone is waiting.' On leaden legs Halina walked slowly towards him and as he took her arm she climbed the steps to the plane.

She'd been on Abkar's royal jet many times before, going to and from school, but it felt different now, walking into Rico's own plane. She glanced around at the sumptuous leather sofas and low coffee tables. Several crew members were waiting attentively, their faces carefully bland. Did they know who she was, that she was pregnant with their employer's child?

Rico strode in behind her and gestured for her to sit down. 'After take-off you can shower and rest. The flight will take approximately six hours.'

Numbly Halina nodded. She felt dazed, unable to process everything that had happened to her. Everything that was going to happen. *Marriage.*

She swallowed hard and looked out at the bright blue sky, the glare of the sun making the tarmac shimmer. The plane began to taxi down the runway and then they were taking off into the sky, away from all she had known.

As soon as they'd reached cruising altitude, Rico rose. 'I'll show you the bedroom.'

Halina followed him, aching with exhaustion, too tired even to think. The bedroom was even more luxurious than the living area, with a king-sized bed on its own dais, built in wardrobes and a huge flat-screen TV.

She gazed around at the adjoining bathroom, complete with a glassed-in shower and marble tub, the furnishings and amenities the height of luxury.

'This is amazing,' she murmured. 'I've never been on such a plane.'

'Not even the royal jet?' Rico returned with a quirk of his eyebrow.

Halina shook her head. 'Not even then.'

He stared at her for a moment, and Halina gazed back, uncertain how to navigate this moment. How to navigate every moment. She couldn't discern what he was thinking, what feelings, what fears or desires, lurked beneath his hard, metallic gaze, if any. Rico Falcone was a completely closed book and she had no idea what its pages held.

'When you're rested and refreshed,' Rico said implacably, 'we'll talk.'

Halina nodded and Rico walked back out to the main cabin, closing the door behind him. She sank onto the bed with a sigh of relief, glad to be alone for a few moments, away from the intensity of Rico's presence. She was desperate to wash, and also to think. To figure out what her next steps were...because Rico certainly knew his.

She spent far longer than necessary in the bath, luxuriating in the hot water and fragrant bubbles. The Palace of Forgotten Sands was forgotten in more ways than one; there had been no updating of its interior in over a hundred years, which meant her washing facilities, along with everything else, had been depressingly basic. A long, lovely soak went a good way to restoring her strength and spirit.

There were clothes in her size in one of the wardrobes, and Halina wondered if Rico had had them chosen specially for her. Or did he simply have a woman's wardrobe on hand for whatever mistress was his flavour of the week?

Pushing the thought out of her mind, she dressed in a pale-blue shift dress that, despite being her usual size, hung off her currently gaunt frame. She'd lost more weight than she'd realised in the last few weeks. Twisting her hair up into a loose bun, Halina squared her shoulders and then went to meet her fate.

Rico was sprawled on one of the sofas, a laptop in front of him, his forehead furrowed in a frown. He looked as sexy and as self-assured as ever, having changed into a knit shirt in charcoal-grey and dark trousers, both garments fitting his body to perfection and emphasising his incredible physique.

He looked up as soon as she entered, and then snapped his fingers. A staff member sprang forward.

'Sparkling water, orange juice and a full breakfast for both of us,' he ordered. 'And I'll have coffee as well.'

'Very good, sir.'

Halina watched as the man hurried to carry out his employer's orders. 'Are all your staff terrified of you?' she asked as she sat down opposite Rico, tucking her legs to the side to avoid his own long outstretched ones. She was determined not to be caught on the back foot, as she had been ever since Rico had stormed into her room at the palace. Now she would regain some control and all her composure. She knew she needed both for whatever lay ahead.

'Why should they be terrified of me?'

'Because you shout at them.'

'I didn't shout.' He looked mildly annoyed by her observation. 'I gave an order. There is a difference.'

'Is there? You don't seem to use "please" or "thank you" the way most people do.'

His mouth compressed. 'I do not like to waste time with useless fripperies, but I can be as polite as the next person.'

Halina looked away, wondering why she was baiting him over such a trivial matter at such a tense and crucial moment. Maybe because she felt so raw, chafing under his endless orders. He fully intended to command her life, and the truth was she didn't think there was anything she could do about it, except perhaps face it head on.

'So.' She squared her shoulders and met his narrowed look directly. 'What do you mean, you're going to marry me in Rome?' Rico regarded Halina and the way she was bracing herself, as if for bad news.

'Exactly that,' he informed her crisply.

'I have to say, your proposal could use some work.'

'I imagine it's a sight better than your last fiancé's,' Rico remarked with a touch of acid, nettled, even though he knew he shouldn't be. 'As I've heard it, you never even met him.'

'No,' Halina said slowly. 'I didn't. Not until a few weeks ago, anyway.'

Rico drew up short at that. He'd known the marriage had been called off, but he hadn't realised Halina had actually seen al bin Nur. 'You saw Prince Zayed recently? Since we…?'

'Yes, *since we*.' Her smile was tinged with wry sorrow. 'When my father found out I was pregnant, he tried to reopen marriage negotiations with Prince Zayed.' Fury flashed through Rico, a lightning strike of emotion he quickly suppressed. So his fears that another man might raise his child had been justified, making him realise how right he'd been to take drastic measures in finding Halina.

'And?' he asked, biting the word off and spitting it out.

'And I refused him, because I didn't want to marry a man who loved another.'

'Who does the Prince love? The governess he kidnapped by accident?' Contempt dripped from every word; how could a man be so unprepared, so foolish, as to abduct the wrong woman and, even worse, fall in love with her? Weakness twice over.

'Yes.' Halina's eyes flashed darkly. 'They fell in

love with each other out in the desert, and I wanted them to be happy. And,' she added, flinging out the word, 'I didn't want to bind myself to someone who could never love me.' There was a challenge in her words, in her eyes, as if daring him to disagree, to disabuse her of such a notion—and so he would, without compunction.

'You were willing to do so before, it seems.'

'I knew Prince Zayed didn't love me before,' Halina clarified, 'but he could have grown to love me in time, as we'd come to know one another. To go into a situation knowing it will never happen…that the man you have bound yourself to for ever will never feel even the smallest affection for you…that is truly hopeless. It is total despair.'

Her words hammered through him, echoing emptily. Rico's mouth twisted. 'And yet here we are,' he observed.

She gave a small, strained smile, the knowledge of their situation clouding and darkening her eyes. 'Yes. Here we are.'

He regarded her closely, trying to gauge her mood. Acceptance, resignation, or something else? 'I take it then you have no objections to our marriage?' he said after a moment, making it not quite a question.

'If you mean will I resist then, no, I won't.' She turned her head to look out of the window, acting as condemned as a prisoner in the dock.

'You will want for nothing,' Rico informed her,

his tone harsher than he'd intended. 'I can promise you that.'

She turned back to stare at him, her expression bleak. 'No, you can't, Rico. You can't promise me anything. You don't know me, and you cannot presume to know either what is in my head or my heart. But if you meant I will live in comfortable circumstances…' She glanced around the plane, appearing deliberately unimpressed despite her earlier comments about the jet's luxury. 'Then, yes, I believe that.'

Rico stared at her, trying to suppress the ever-deepening twinge of annoyance her words caused. He shouldn't care what she thought or felt, only that she wasn't going to protest their inevitable marriage. Yet somehow her attitude of resignation rankled, as if he were marching her towards a noose rather than down an aisle.

'I'm glad to hear you will not attempt some pointless protest.'

She let out a huff of humourless laughter. 'Exactly. It would be pointless. My life has never been my own. I suppose it doesn't matter much whether it is you or my father who is pulling the strings.'

'I think it would matter at least a little,' Rico returned. 'As my wife you will certainly have some freedom and autonomy. More, I think, than you would have had otherwise, should you have married Prince Zayed or stayed in your father's home.'

Halina's eyes flashed dark fire. 'Prison is prison, no matter how gilded the cage.'

Although it wasn't an avenue of discussion he really wanted to explore, Rico could not keep from asking, 'What is the alternative, Halina? You are carrying my child. What would you propose, if not marriage?' He thought of the way she'd hidden from him. 'Would you really want to live the rest of your life out in the desert to escape me?'

She was silent for a long moment, gazing out of the window at the azure sky, her expression thoughtful and a little sad. Rico felt himself getting tenser and tenser. *What was she thinking?* And why did he want to know so badly?

'When I was a little girl,' Halina began slowly, 'I had this daydream. I wanted to live in Paris, in one of those tall, old houses, like Madeleine in the children's story. Do you know those books?' Wordlessly Rico shook his head. 'I had them as a child, given to me by my French godmother. I loved them.' She lapsed into silence and Rico waited, having no idea where she was going with this.

'I pictured it all in my head,' she continued in a dreamy, faraway voice. 'I used to decorate it in my imagination. I'd live on the top floor, and there would be vines climbing outside and big French windows that opened onto a balcony with wrought-iron railings. I'd grow flowers and herbs in pots and I'd sit outside and sip my coffee and look at the world bustling below.' She smiled, caught in the memory, and Rico stared at her, bewildered. He had no idea what to say. What to think.

'And there was a piano in the living room,' Halina continued. 'A grand piano that I played on. I'd give music lessons as well, and I'd have a tin of sweets on top of the piano to hand out to children when they were good. And when I wasn't working I'd go outside and wander through the Tuileries Gardens—they were mentioned in the Madeleine books as well—and sketch.' She glanced up at him, a hint of a smile in her eyes. 'Do you know, I've never actually been to Paris? This is all just in my dreams.'

'Perhaps you'll visit there one day,' Rico said gruffly. 'With me.'

'Perhaps.' Halina turned back to the window. 'The thing is,' she said softly, 'I always knew I'd never live that dream. I'd never even have the chance. I've never had any say in my life, Rico. That's why I went to the party that night in Rome. The night I met you.' She drew a shuddering breath. 'I just wanted one evening to myself, to make my own choices.' She let out a hollow laugh. 'And look what a disaster that was. Perhaps my father was right all along in restricting my life so much. Maybe I'm not capable of making my own choices, or at least wise ones. But I've always wanted the chance. I still do.'

Her words resonated uncomfortably inside him, because in a strange way he could relate to them. His childhood had been entirely different to Halina's; she'd been cossetted, protected, privileged. He'd grown up first on the docks and then in the orphanage, both places of nothing more than grim survival. And yet he'd felt as trapped and restricted as she had, and his only choice had been to fight his way out. To be seen as cold, arrogant, ruthless. Because at least then he was in control. At least then he couldn't be hurt.

What was Halina's choice?

She didn't need one, Rico reminded himself. He would provide for her, protect her, give her every luxury she could possibly want. All this nonsense about an apartment in Paris was just a childish dream, meant to be discarded and forgotten upon adulthood.

Their breakfasts arrived, putting an end to any more whimsical conversation.

'You need to eat,' Rico reminded her as he watched Halina push the eggs around her plate. 'Keep up your strength.'

'I know.' She took a tiny bite of dry toast. 'I've just been feeling so ill.'

Which reminded him that she hadn't yet seen a doctor. 'As soon as we arrive in Rome, I want you to be checked over. I'm sure something can be prescribed for your nausea.'

'Hopefully,' Halina murmured, her gaze downcast. She took another bite of toast. Rico regarded her in growing frustration, unsure why he felt so dissatisfied.

He'd found her, he'd got her on the plane and they were now only mere hours from Rome. She'd already agreed to marry him. He was getting everything he wanted, and still he felt disgruntled and annoyed. *Hurt.*

The word popped into his head and he suppressed it immediately. He wasn't hurt. He never felt hurt. He'd never allowed himself to feel such a thing, not since his father had walked away from him while he'd watched. If he was bothered by Halina's lukewarm response to the idea of their marriage, then he knew just how to rev up her enthusiasm.

In bed.

CHAPTER EIGHT

HALINA TOOK A deep breath as she gazed at her pale reflection in the mirror the morning after her arrival in Rome. The last twenty-four hours had been a whirlwind of activity and movement: a limousine had met them at the airport and taken them to Rico's penthouse apartment in a sleekly elegant modern building near the Spanish Steps.

Halina had stepped into the sprawling luxury, too tired to be dazzled or impressed by the striking minimalist architecture and hand-crafted pieces of furniture. She'd felt as if she were a tiny boat being tossed on an endless stormy sea and Rico was the one controlling the wind and the waves.

As soon as they'd arrived he had shown her to the guest bedroom and practically ordered her to rest. For once Halina had been glad to obey. She was so tired she was swaying on her feet.

'Will you tell my father where I am?' she'd asked as she stood on the threshold of her bedroom. 'So at least he won't worry?'

Rico had given a terse nod, his expression flinty.

'I think he already knows, but I will inform him of our plans at a suitable time.'

'And when will that be?'

Rico had shrugged. 'When I decide it is.'

Of course. He decided everything. She'd turned into the bedroom and closed the door in Rico's face. At least she had control over that.

Six hours of sleep later, Halina was feeling refreshed physically even as her emotions remained wrung out. She lay in bed and relived the last twenty-four hours—the escape from the palace, the terrifying sandstorm, the flight to Rome. It all felt incredible, almost as if it had happened to someone else, scenes out of an action film or a melodrama. Until she'd met Rico Falcone, her life had been quiet, contained and definitely dull. Now, she acknowledged wryly, it was merely contained.

By the time she awoke from her nap, dusk was falling over the city. Rico knocked on her door, telling her she needed to eat, which seemed to be his constant refrain. Halina went out and managed to choke down some soup before retreating to bed before Rico could ask her any more questions or give her any more orders.

'I have made an appointment for you to see a doctor tomorrow morning,' he informed her as she headed for her bedroom. 'You need to start taking better care of yourself.'

She didn't trust herself to answer in a civil manner, so she merely nodded. Alone in bed that night, misery rushed over her. She'd thought being locked away in a palace in the remote desert of Abkar had been bad enough, but amazingly this actually felt worse. She was so alone. Rico was a hostile stranger who seemed intent on blaming her for everything, yet still intended her to marry him. What would her life be like with Rico? What would her child's life be like?

For a few seconds Halina imagined resisting. Running away, carving some kind of life for herself. But where would she go, and what would she do? She had no money, no clothes even, and her life skills were, she knew, pitiable. She could speak three languages, play two instruments and make sparkling conversation when required. They were not exactly qualifications for making her own way in the world.

She hated feeling so trapped. Yet her one bid to escape her gilded shackles had resulted in her ruin, so she hardly trusted herself to try again, even if she could have worked up the courage or the means.

'Halina?' Rico knocked on the door of her bedroom, startling her out of her gloomy thoughts. 'We leave in twenty minutes for the doctor.'

'All right.' She turned away from her wan reflection and opened the door. Rico stood there, looking both glorious and impatient, dressed in a pin-striped suit in deep navy, his eyes glinting like metal, his jaw freshly shaven and his hair spiky and slightly damp from the shower. He smelled of sandalwood, and the scent of him hit Halina like a fist squeezing her heart.

She remembered his hands on her body all over again, the honeyed persuasion of his kiss.

With effort she yanked her gaze away from him and walked past him into the living room. 'I'm ready.'

'I sent out for some things I thought you might like to eat.' Halina turned, surprised to see a flash of uncertainty on Rico's rugged features. She didn't think she'd ever seen him look that way before.

'Thank you.'

'There are some pastries and fresh fruit, and also ginger tea. I read that ginger helps with nausea.'

Surprise rippled through her. 'You've been reading up on it?'

He shrugged. 'I want to know as much as I can. Information is vital.'

'Thank you,' Halina said again. She felt strangely touched by his concern, although another part of her acknowledged how little it was in the larger scheme of things. But maybe she'd just have to get used to little, at least in terms of affection or concern. Rico hardly seemed likely to offer anything else.

Rome was shimmering under a haze of heat as they stepped outside Rico's apartment. He held open the door of the limousine and she slid inside, edging to the far side as Rico sat next to her, seeming to take up all the space and air. Heat emanated from his powerful body and strength radiated from every taut muscle. The sheer power of his charisma left her breathless. She'd forgotten how overwhelming he was, and she was reminded again and again of that fact every time she went near him. It was no wonder she hadn't been able to resist him back at that party.

'So, do you live in Rome all the time?' she asked as the limo pulled smoothly into the traffic. 'I don't actually know that much about you.' Or anything, really, except that he was rich, ruthless and arrogant. *And fabulous in bed.*

'Most of the time.' Rico swiped his phone and slid it into his pocket, giving her his full attention, which felt like stepping into a spotlight. 'I travel for business to my various concerns and properties, most of which are in Europe.'

'Your penthouse isn't really suitable for a baby,' Halina said impulsively. 'Would I live there?'

Rico stared at her for a moment, his expression unfathomable. 'Of course we will need to work out the details, but I would most likely buy a house in Rome suitable for a family.'

For a second Halina let herself imagine it—a happy home, a place she could decorate and fill with music and art, books and laughter. A place of her own, of their own, where she and Rico could learn to live and maybe even love together. But of course it wouldn't be like that. How it would be, she didn't yet know.

'And when will we marry?' she asked eventually. The silence between them had become strained, tense, as it always seemed to.

Rico looked out of the window. 'Let's concentrate

on today and making sure you and our child are both healthy. After that we can focus on the wedding.'

The doctor's office was upscale and comfortable, with a staff member fluttering around them making sure they had everything they needed, including fresh juice and coffee.

Halina's nerves started to jangle as she stepped into the examining room with Rico right behind her. The doctor smiled at her and introduced herself.

'My name is Maria Loretto. Signor Falcone has engaged me to be your obstetrician.'

Halina nodded and shook her hand. 'Thank you.'

'So the first thing we need to do is ascertain how far along you are.' Maria gestured for her to sit on the examining table, and nervously Halina perched on its end. 'If you know the date of your last period…'

'We know the date of conception,' Rico interjected flatly. Halina closed her eyes. Did he have to control this too?

Maria glanced up. 'If you're sure of it…'

'I'm sure. It was June twenty-fifth.'

Colour scorched Halina's cheeks and she stayed silent while Maria calculated her due date. 'So you are just over ten weeks along,' she said cheerfully. 'And your due date is March nineteenth.'

Halina let out a shaky laugh and instinctively pressed one hand against her still-flat middle. Somehow just those words made it feel so much more real. For the last two months she'd been merely existing, feeling wretched and uncertain and afraid, barely able to contemplate what was ahead of her. But now the reality, the good reality, of her situation hit her with encouraging force. A baby. A child.

'Now we can check the heartbeat,' Maria continued. 'You're just far enough along perhaps to hear it with a Doppler. Would you mind lying down?'

Halina lay back on the examining table, feeling weirdly vulnerable as Maria lifted her top. She switched on the Doppler and then pressed the wand onto Halina's stomach, hard enough to make her flinch.

'You're hurting her.' The words seemed to burst out of Rico; he looked tense, almost angry, his jaw clenched. Unfazed, the doctor gave him a reassuring smile.

'Halina is fine, Signor Falcone, and babies are remarkably resilient.'

Rico still looked unhappy about it and Halina reached out one hand, almost but not quite touching him. 'I'm fine, Rico.'

He nodded once and then they heard it, the most amazing sound Halina had ever listened to. It sounded like a cross between the whooshing of waves and the galloping of a horse. Their baby's heartbeat.

'There it is,' Maria said with satisfaction. 'Nice and strong.'

'That's amazing.' Halina felt near to tears, but when she turned to look at Rico, instinctively wanting to share this moment with him, he'd turned away as if he wasn't affected at all.

"FAST FIVE" READER SURVEY

Your participation entitles you to:
✳ **4 Thank-You Gifts Worth Over $20!**

Complete the survey in minutes.

Get **2 FREE** Books

Your Thank-You Gifts include **2 FREE BOOKS** and **2 MYSTERY GIFTS**. There's no obligation to purchase anything!

See inside for details.

Dear Reader,

Since you are a lover of our books, your opinions are important to us... and so is your time.

That's why we made sure your **"FAST FIVE" READER SURVEY** can be completed in just a few minutes. Your answers to the five questions will help us remain at the forefront of women's fiction.

And, as a thank-you for participating, we'd like to send you **4 FREE THANK-YOU GIFTS!**

Enjoy your gifts with our appreciation,

Pam Powers

To get your
4 FREE THANK-YOU GIFTS:

✴ Quickly complete the "Fast Five" Reader Survey
and return the insert.

"FAST FIVE" READER SURVEY

1 Do you sometimes read a book a second or third time? ○ Yes ○ No

2 Do you often choose reading over other forms of entertainment such as television? ○ Yes ○ No

3 When you were a child, did someone regularly read aloud to you? ○ Yes ○ No

4 Do you sometimes take a book with you when you travel outside the home? ○ Yes ○ No

5 In addition to books, do you regularly read newspapers and magazines? ○ Yes ○ No

YES! I have completed the above Reader Survey. Please send me my 4 FREE GIFTS (gifts worth over $20 retail). I understand that I am under no obligation to buy anything, as explained on the back of this card.

❏ I prefer the regular-print edition
106/306 HDL GM3S

❏ I prefer the larger-print edition
176/376 HDL GM3S

FIRST NAME	LAST NAME

ADDRESS

APT.#	CITY

STATE/PROV.	ZIP/POSTAL CODE

◄ If offer card is missing write to: Reader Service, P.O. Box 1341, Buffalo, NY 14240-8531 or visit www.ReaderService.com ►

BUSINESS REPLY MAIL
FIRST-CLASS MAIL   PERMIT NO. 717   BUFFALO, NY

POSTAGE WILL BE PAID BY ADDRESSEE

READER SERVICE
PO BOX 1341
BUFFALO NY 14240-8571

NO POSTAGE
NECESSARY
IF MAILED
IN THE
UNITED STATES

* * *

The sound seemed to fill the room, rushing and strong, the sound of hope. Rico clenched his jaw, forcing the sudden and unexpected rush of emotion back. It was just a sound, yet it filled him with joy and terror in equal measures. Their child. A human being that they had created, that he would be responsible for. That he would love.

He glanced at Halina out of the corner of his eye and saw how moved she looked, her eyes bright with tears. No matter how much he wanted to keep things on a businesslike level between them, this was an emotional business for them both. How could it be otherwise?

'Halina's been feeling very nauseous,' he told the obstetrician, his voice terser than he meant it to be. 'As you can see, she hasn't been taking care of herself.' Halina sucked in a quick breath and belatedly Rico realised how that sounded. But he was *worried*, damn it, and he didn't like being worried.

'I can prescribe something for the nausea,' Maria said. 'But first I'd advise fresh air, plenty of rest and lots of good, wholesome food. Have you been able to have all those recently, Halina?'

Was there a knowledgeable glint in the doctor's eye? Rico hadn't informed her of their circumstances, and he didn't like the thought of her knowing.

'Not exactly,' Halina murmured.

'But she will now,' Rico said firmly. Taking care

of Halina would be his priority. Taking care of his unborn child.

'Then I'd suggest you come back to me in a week or two, Halina,' Maria said. 'And we'll discuss medication then. You do look a bit run down.'

She smiled sympathetically and Halina nodded and rose from the table, pulling down her shirt. 'All right. Thank you.' Her head was bowed, her dark hair swinging in front of her face. Rico had no idea what she was thinking. Feeling.

Why did he care?

Because of their baby. For the sake of his child, he needed to care about Halina. About her moods as well as her health. It was all part of the same package. Satisfied with his reasoning, he took her arm as he thanked the doctor and then escorted her out of the building into the waiting limo.

'What now?' Halina asked listlessly as she stared out of the window at the city streaming by. Rico wished she didn't sound so damned downtrodden. When he'd met her, he'd been as intrigued by her humour and spirit as he had been by her lush, curvy body. Now both were gone and he wanted to bring back the Halina he'd only just come to know—bring back the sparkle in her eyes, the impish smile to her mouth and, yes, the curves on the woman whose body had made his palms itch to touch her.

But bringing a smile to her face felt like the most important thing right now.

'What would you like to do now?' Rico asked,

seeming to surprise them both. She turned to him, her eyes widening, jaw dropping in shock.

'You're asking me what I want?'

'Why shouldn't I?'

'Because you're King of the World, Maker of All Decisions Ever?'

'That is a slight exaggeration.' His mouth twitched; he was heartened to see even that little display of spirit. 'But only slight.'

'Of course.'

'Perhaps I should put that on my business card. It's quite catchy, as a title.'

Her mouth curved just a little. 'You're joking with me.'

'Shouldn't I?'

'No, it's just…' Her smile faded. 'I don't know you, Rico, at all. And yet you're the father of my child and soon you're likely to be my husband.'

'There's no likely about it,' Rico couldn't keep from saying, his voice hardening, that moment of levity vanishing like morning mist.

Halina sighed and turned back to the window. 'Exactly.'

Frustration boiled within him. Why could he never get this right? He wasn't used to feeling wrong-footed, unsure, wanting something he couldn't have. 'So what is it you'd like to do today?'

She shrugged, her face still to the window. 'I don't care.'

He found he hated her apathy. 'I'm giving you a choice, Halina—'

'Oh, that's right.' She whirled to face him, a sudden and surprising fury lighting her eyes and twisting her features. 'You're *giving* me a choice. I suppose I should trip all over myself to say thank you for that unimaginable kindness.' He opened his mouth to speak but found he had nothing to say. 'And tomorrow, perhaps, you won't give me a choice. Tomorrow I'll be informed of our plans without any discussion and expected to fall in line immediately *or else.*'

'You are talking about something that hasn't happened yet.'

'You don't get it, do you?' She shook her head in weary despair. 'You never will. I tried to explain before, but you're so used to ordering the universe you can't imagine what it feels like to be the one ordered about. And as privileged as my life has been—and I'm not stupid… I know it has—it's also always been ordered and arranged by someone else. So if you want to know what I want today, Rico, I'll tell you. I want my freedom, and that is something you'll never give me.' She broke off, breathing heavily, turning back to the window as she struggled to compose herself.

Rico sat back, stunned speechless by her outburst. Yes, he understood her life had been restricted and that she resented that, but he hadn't realised how bitterly she chafed against it, against *him*. How she now saw him as her captor, her commander. And he suddenly felt sympathy for her that was both overwhelming and inconvenient.

'Actually,' he said after a moment, keeping his voice mild, 'I do know what that feels like.'

Halina let out a huff of disbelieving laughter, her face still turned firmly towards the window. 'Yeah, right.'

'As you said yourself just a few moments ago, you don't actually know me. So how can you say whether I've felt something or not?'

She stayed silent for a long moment and then she turned towards him. Her face was still flushed, but that moment of furious rebellion had left her, and bizarrely Rico found he missed it. 'Tell me, then.'

But did he actually want to tell her? This was all becoming a bit too…intimate. Rico hesitated, debating the pros and cons of admitting something of his past to her. Then he decided he could tell her. He just wouldn't get emotional about it.

'Well?' Halina lifted her chin, a challenge in her dark gaze. 'Are you going to tell me or not?'

CHAPTER NINE

HALINA SAW THE indecision flicker in Rico's silvery eyes and knew he was regretting admitting even as little as he had to her. He didn't want her to know him. Didn't want to be known.

'For all my childhood, I had little control,' he said at last, his voice toneless. 'Over anything.'

'Most children have little control,' Halina answered with a shrug, determined not to trip all over herself in eager gratitude now that he was sharing something with her. 'Isn't that the nature of childhood?'

'I suppose it is.' His jaw was tight, his eyes flinty. Perhaps she shouldn't have been so dismissive simply because she was frustrated and feeling trapped. She did want to know more about the man she was going to marry, and if Rico was willing to open up even a little she wanted and needed to encourage that.

'How was your childhood different, Rico?' she asked in a gentler tone. 'What was it like?' She really did want to know, and she was sorry for her flippancy.

His lips compressed, his gaze turning distant. 'As

it happens,' he remarked in a cool, matter-of-fact tone, 'I never knew my mother. She was a waitress who had a fling with my father. She didn't want the baby— me—and so she left me with my father when I was two weeks old.'

'Oh.' The word was a soft gasp of sorrow. She had assumed, she realised, that Rico was from as great a world of privilege as her own. He certainly acted as if he had always been entitled, had always expected obedience, or even obeisance. She'd had no idea that he'd been born in such lowly, unfortunate circumstances.

'Yes, oh.' His mouth twisted with wry grimness. 'My father worked on the docks, and I don't think he was best pleased to have a baby foisted on him, even his own.'

'Oh,' Halina said again, helplessly. 'That must have been… What did he do?'

'He kept me, to his credit.' Rico flicked his gaze away for a second before he turned resolutely back to face her, his face bland. 'Raised me himself, with help from some kindly neighbours who looked after me when I was small.' His lips thinned. 'It could have been worse.'

'So you never knew your mother at all? You grew up with your father?'

'Until I was nine.' Rico shrugged, as if to dismiss the matter. 'Then I ended up in an orphanage in Salerno. A convent, run by nuns who didn't like children very much, as far as I could tell. That's where

I really grew up. I left when I was sixteen and never looked back.'

Sadness clutched at Halina's heart. It sounded like a truly miserable childhood—not a childhood at all. 'Oh, Rico, that sounds horrible. So lonely—'

'I've never been lonely.' He cut across her. 'I've never needed to feel lonely, because long ago I learned to depend only on myself.' He paused, adding a certain emphasis to the words, making her realise that he wasn't just talking about his childhood. He was talking about now, about not needing anyone now. Not needing her.

'But the real reason I told you all this,' Rico resumed, 'is to explain that I do know how you feel when you say you're trapped and want freedom.'

Halina flushed and looked down. It sounded as if Rico's life had been far more restricted than hers had ever been. She felt ashamed, a spoilt princess whingeing for even more than she already had. 'I'm sorry for doubting you. I never would have guessed… How did you get to where you are now?'

'Determination, hard work and a little bit of luck. Perhaps more than a little bit.' His eyes flashed with fire. 'I bought my first property when I was nineteen, a rundown warehouse near the docks, and turned it into a gym. I sold it for twenty times what I paid for it when I was twenty-one and then never looked back.'

Halina shook her head slowly. 'That is truly amazing, Rico. You're an inspiration.'

He gave a nod of acknowledgement and thanks.

'So, now I shall ask you again. What would you like to do this afternoon?'

Halina stared at him thoughtfully, wondering what she could suggest that Rico would agree to, that could be fun for them both. Because now that he'd shared something of his life, that surprising insight into a difficult childhood, she realised she wanted to spend time with him. To get to know him, to crack open the door into his mind, if not his heart, and gain another tantalising glimpse.

If they were going to be married, she needed to know this man. Understand him and hopefully even like him.

'What do you recommend?' she asked. 'I spent all my secondary schooling in Italy, but I've never actually seen any sights.'

'That's tragic.'

'Have you?' she challenged and his lips twitched.

'I'm too busy to sightsee.'

'Of course you are. But today...?'

He glanced out of the window, his expression as thoughtful as her own. 'We could see the Colosseum. That's something I've always wanted to visit.'

Halina's heart leapt with excitement and a strange hope. This was new, doing something together just for fun. Not sex, not squabbling, just simple pleasure, spending time with each other. 'All right,' she said. 'Let's see that.'

Rico insisted on lunch first, so they ate in the private garden of an elegant bistro only steps from the

Colosseum. The food was fresh and delicious, a refreshing breeze ruffling the leaves of the plane trees that offered some much-needed shade.

Halina sat back as they waited for their food, feeling surprisingly happy for the first time in months. Maybe even longer. Her heart was light, anticipation burgeoning inside her.

'You're smiling,' Rico noted as he twirled his wine glass between long, lean fingers.

'I am, actually,' she admitted as her smile widened. 'This is very nice, Rico. Thank you.'

'You're welcome.' He tilted his head, his silvery, heavy-lidded gaze sweeping over her in assessment, considering. 'You're quite easily pleased, you know.'

'Do you really think so?' Halina took a sip of her sparkling water. 'I suppose, after the last few months, I am.'

Rico's eyes narrowed. 'What does that mean exactly?'

Halina bit her lip and looked away. 'It doesn't really matter.' She didn't want to drag up all those painful memories, only to have Rico question and doubt her and definitely spoil the fun but fragile mood that had begun to develop between them.

'And I think it does.' He leaned forward, as intent as a predator on its prey, and just as lethal. 'You have never told me about the time between your visits to Rome. Why you didn't see a doctor. How you ended up in that remote palace.'

'I thought you believed I'd gone there to escape

from you,' Halina returned. She'd meant to sound light but a note of bitterness crept in. How could he have made so many assumptions? But how could she be surprised that he had?

'It was the first thought that came to my mind,' Rico acknowledged. 'But perhaps that is because of my experience, not yours. Now I'd like to hear in your own words how you came to be at that palace.' He paused, gazing down into the glinting ruby depths of his wine. 'How did your family take the news of your pregnancy?'

'Not well.' The two words scraped Halina's throat and she took another sip of water. 'Not well at all, to be perfectly frank.'

Rico frowned. 'I thought your father doted on you.'

She laughed, the sound rather grim. 'Where did you hear that?'

'I hired a private investigator to find you. He found that the general sense was that your father doted on you, and that you were rather spoiled.' His gaze, when she dared to meet it, was steady and clear, without judgement or pity. 'Is that true?'

'It *was* true,' Halina said after a moment, when she trusted her voice to be as steady as his gaze. 'But it all changed when I ruined myself.'

Rico's eyebrows drew together in a straight line, his frown turning into a scowl so that he looked quite ferocious. 'Tell me what happened.'

'What I should have expected would happen,' Halina answered with a shrug. Even now she couldn't believe how stupid, how utterly naive, she'd been, and in so many ways. About Rico, about her father, about life. 'My parents were beyond furious with me. When the negotiations with Prince Zayed broke down, my father had been hoping to marry me to someone else, someone he deemed suitable, who would afford us another political alliance. My disgrace precluded that.'

'Surely in this day and age a woman's virginity is not a prerequisite, even for a royal marriage?'

'In my country, in my culture, it is. And I knew that.' She shook her head. 'All along I knew that, and yet still I acted as if the consequences wouldn't apply to me.' She tried for a twisted smile. 'I suppose you truly did sweep me away, Rico.'

'It was mutual,' Rico said after a brief pause. 'If I'd had any sense myself, any ability to think straight, I would have realised how innocent you were. And I wouldn't have touched you.'

'Was it that obvious?'

'In hindsight, yes. So what did your father do?'

'He was livid with me, first of all. Utterly enraged, as well as disappointed. I'm not sure which felt worse.' She shook her head, the memories assailing her like hammer blows. 'And when he found out I was pregnant...'

'How did he find out, as a matter of interest?'

'He made me take a pregnancy test,' Halina said simply. 'At the earliest opportunity. And then he tried to have Prince Zayed marry me, spoiled goods that I was, because he didn't think anyone else would have me. And when that didn't work out...' She gulped, not wanting to go on, closing her eyes against the harshness of the memory that still hurt her even now.

'What?' Rico demanded roughly. 'Whatever it is, tell me, Halina. Surely it can't be worse than another man claiming my child?'

She saw how the skin around his lips had gone white, his eyes hard and metallic. He was angry, but with her father, not with her. Would he be even angrier when she told him the whole truth?

'You have to understand,' Halina said slowly. 'My father is a good man. A loving man.' She had to believe that, because if she didn't what did she have? A father who had never actually truly loved her? 'But,' she continued painfully, 'he was in very difficult circumstances...'

'It sounds as if you were in very difficult circumstances,' Rico interjected shortly.

Yes, she had been, but the circumstances had been of her own making. And she supposed she wanted to explain her father's actions—absolve him, even—because she still loved him and wanted to believe he loved her. Otherwise, what was love, that he could be doting one minute and damning the next? How did you trust it, if it could so easily turn into something else? What was love, if you couldn't forgive a mistake, an insult, an open wound?

'Halina,' Rico said, and it sounded like a warning.

'He tried,' Halina confessed in a low voice, 'To make me have an abortion.'

* * *

Rico stared at Halina, her pale face, her pain-filled eyes, and felt a whole new kind of fury sweep through him—a tidal wave of anger and indignation and, beneath those, a deep, soul-reaching pain.

'He tried?' he repeated in a growl. 'What do you mean by that?'

'He insisted, and he wouldn't listen to me at all. My mother agreed with him, and they took me to a discreet doctor. Forced me.' She blinked rapidly but a tear fell anyway, glistening on her cheek like a diamond. Rico's fists clenched on the table. 'I fought the whole way, tooth and nail.' She stared at him, her eyes huge. 'You have to believe that, Rico. I would never want to get rid of my child. I begged and pleaded, I cried and fought. I did.' She let out a choked cry, one trembling fist pressed to her mouth.

'I do believe it,' he said in a low voice. It was impossible not to when he could feel her desperation and grief like a tangible thing, a shroud covering her. 'So, what happened then?'

'The doctor refused to perform the operation,' Halina whispered. 'Because I was fighting against it so much. My father was furious, but in the midst of it all I think he saw where his own anger had led him, and he was ashamed.' She swiped at the tear still glistening on her cheek. 'I have to believe that.'

And Rico understood that too, because he'd felt the same about his own father for many years, trying to excuse the inexcusable, to give a good reason for cruelty towards a child. Towards him. You could twist the truth into knots to try to make it an acceptable shape, but it all came apart eventually, and he'd had to acknowledge the hard, unvarnished reality. His father just hadn't cared.

'So he sent you to the Palace of Forgotten Sands,' Rico said flatly. 'He banished you.'

Halina nodded, swallowing hard in an attempt to restore her shaky composure. 'Yes, I was meant to remain there until the baby was born.'

'And afterwards?'

'I…I don't know.' Halina bit her lip. 'My father said he would take my baby away from me, but I hoped… I hoped in time he would change his mind and let me keep him or her.' She pressed one hand to her belly. 'I can't believe he would have been so cruel to me or his own grandchild.'

Rico sat back, his mind whirling with all the revelations Halina had just levelled at him. He'd misjudged her badly, assuming she'd been acting on her own selfish whims, going to a remote location to keep his child from him. It had been a stupid assumption, founded on his own unfortunate experience and the ensuing prejudices he still had about mothers and fathers, about family, about love.

Because he'd never experienced a mother's love, a father's trust. Because he'd assumed Halina would act in as selfish and capricious a manner as his own mother had done. He'd been wrong. So very wrong.

'I'm sorry you went through all that,' he said finally. 'And I'm sorry I assumed…' He paused, realising how much he'd assumed. How much it must have hurt her, considering her true experience. 'I'm sorry,' he said again.

Halina nodded, pale-faced and spent now. 'That's why I didn't see an obstetrician,' she explained quietly. 'I wasn't given the chance.'

'I understand.' Rico spoke tautly, trying to control the raging anger he felt towards Halina's father. The man had no right to assume control over Halina's life, over their child's life. The thought that Halina might have been forced to terminate her pregnancy—end the life of his child—made Rico grind his teeth together. But his rage served no purpose now, not when Halina was looking at him so warily, as if afraid his anger might be directed at her. And why shouldn't she be afraid? Since snatching her from the desert palace, he'd assumed the worst of her at nearly every turn. Guilt, an unfamiliar emotion, lanced through him.

From the depths of his soul, a barren landscape until now, Rico summoned a smile. 'Let's put such unpleasant things behind us, Halina. The future will be different now—for you and for our baby, who will never know a day without the love of his or her mother and father. That is my promise.'

Halina nodded, but she didn't look much convinced, something which made guilt rush through Rico all over again. He could see now how arrogant and inconsiderate he'd been—announcing his dictates, never giving her a choice—and he vowed to do better in the future. He would provide for Halina, he would make her smile, he would see her blossom, so she could rediscover her old spirit and joy.

He just would do it without engaging any of his own emotions. Because even now, when his heart was nearly rent in two by Halina's sorrowful story, Rico steeled himself not to care. That was one place he could not go, and one thing he would never, ever give his bride-to-be. His heart. Even now, having shared and been entrusted with so much, he couldn't risk that much.

They spent the rest of lunch talking about inconsequential matters, then strolled through the sunshine to the Colosseum.

'Photographs don't do it justice!' Halina exclaimed as they walked through an archway, one of eighty. Although partially ruined, the Colosseum was still a magnificent and awe-inspiring structure with its high walls and many archways, the expanse of the old arena.

They roamed through its many corridors, reading each other bits from the guidebook—how it had been built by three different emperors and then had fallen to ruin a few hundred years later, much of its stone used to build other structures in Rome.

'It's horrible and beautiful all at once, isn't it?' Halina said as they stood on the viewing platform that overlooked what had once been the main arena. 'The architecture is so impressive, and yet so many people and animals suffered and died here terribly. It's awful to think about.'

Rico nodded. 'Beautiful things can be used for evil,' he said, feeling strangely sombre after their walk around the ancient archways and corridors. He felt as if he was sharing more than a mere tourist attraction with Halina; the way they'd talked together, reflecting on what they'd learned in the guidebook, was something he'd never done with a woman before, or really with anyone.

He didn't have friends, not beyond business colleagues, and women had been no more than mistresses, mere objects of sexual desire and fulfillment. Strolling in the sunshine on a summer's afternoon, sharing ideas, talking and listening, was all incredibly novel. And, he realised with a pang of unease, quite pleasant, which he hadn't expected at all.

He'd been viewing this afternoon as an expedient means to an end, a way to improve Halina's mood, gain her trust. But somewhere along the way it had turned into something else, something deeper and more meaningful, and he really didn't know how to feel about that because, the truth was, he didn't want to *feel* at all.

Halina glanced down at the guidebook. 'It says we shouldn't miss the museum in the inner walls of the top floor,' she remarked. 'It's dedicated to Eros.'

'Eros?'

'The god of love.'

'I know who Eros is,' Rico returned. 'I just don't know why they'd have a museum dedicated to him in a place that was used for torture and death.'

'Maybe that's why, to bring some light and hope to a place that has been the stage for so much darkness.' Halina's smile was teasing and playful, but her eyes looked serious and Rico felt a twinge of alarm, a deepening sense of unease.

Love did not bring light to the darkness; it wasn't the hope held out in a broken and damaged world. No, love was nothing but risk and pain, loss and weakness. He knew that because he'd made the grievous mistake of loving his father. A broken childhood might not be the best reason to avoid love, but it was Rico's, and it had affected him to the depths of his soul. It had made him determined not just to avoid love but revile it and all it meant. Because the alternative was unthinkable. Unbearable.

As he took Halina's arm and led her towards the stairs, Rico sincerely hoped that she wasn't holding out for some remnant of love from him. Surely she knew him better than that, even if their acquaintance had been limited so far?

If she didn't know it, he reflected grimly, he would certainly tell her as soon as possible, gently but firmly. He didn't want to hurt Halina any more than he already had, but the last thing he needed or wanted was a wife who was looking for that damnable emotion—love.

CHAPTER TEN

HALINA GAZED AT her reflection in the mirror, noting
the colour in her cheeks, the new sparkle in her eyes.
It had been two weeks since she'd arrived in Rome
with Rico and the nausea was finally abating, thanks
to plenty of rest, healthy food and fresh air, as well
as simple time. She was nearly at the end of her first
trimester, and her pregnancy—her baby—was becoming more real with every passing day.

The last two weeks had been surprisingly unpres-
sured. Rico had been focused on restoring her health,
and Halina had appreciated the chance to take long
naps and baths, or simply sit out in the sun on the
huge terrace off Rico's apartment. He'd hired a cook
to make fresh, nourishing meals and had cancelled all
his social engagements so he could be home as much
as possible in the evenings after work.

He was acting every inch the loving, considerate
husband except…he wasn't. After that first shocking
conversation when he'd told her about his childhood,
Rico had buttoned up, sharing no personal details, in-
viting no intimate conversations. Halina had missed

it, had tried several times to engage him again, but any questions about his childhood, his feelings, his very self, had been firmly and sometimes brusquely shot down. Halina had a suspicion he regretted sharing as much as he had with her, and this was his way of retrenching.

That had been most apparent when they'd visited the museum dedicated to Eros at the Colosseum. They'd strolled through the galleries of frescoes and sculpture, terracotta vases and bas-reliefs, while Halina had read from the guidebook.

'The ancient poets describe Eros as an invincible force that can bring happiness but also destroy it.'

Rico had snorted, his hands shoved deep in his pockets. 'The latter is certainly true.'

Halina had glanced at him over the edge of the guidebook. 'You sound as if you've been in love,' she'd remarked, trying not to feel an inconvenient twinge of jealousy at the thought. Was that why he kept to mistresses, none of whom lasted longer than a week? To keep his heart from being broken again?

'Not *in* love,' Rico had corrected, then had refused to say anything more.

'I've never been in love,' Halina had remarked with an insouciant shrug. 'Never even close. Never had the chance.'

'Consider yourself fortunate, then.'

'What have you got against it?' She tried to keep her voice light, to disguise the hurt and, yes, the yearning she knew she felt. She might never have been in love but she wanted to be one day. And if she married Rico, *when* she married him, it seemed likely that she wouldn't be.

'You heard what the ancient poets said.' Rico paused to study a statue of Eros stringing his bow. 'It can destroy happiness. Who wants to tangle with that? And what about the whole concept of love being an arrow that hits you?' He nodded towards the marble figure. 'Something that is alleged to bring joy actually brings pain. That sounds about right.'

Halina stopped where she was and lowered the guidebook. 'Who hurt you, Rico?' she asked quietly. He jerked as if shot by the aforementioned arrow, his eyes narrowed.

'No one.'

'That can't be true, not with the way you're talking.'

He shrugged one powerful shoulder. 'It was a long time ago.'

'How long ago?'

'I don't want to talk about it, Halina.' His tone couldn't have been more repressive, and Halina didn't have the courage to press any more. But she wondered. Oh, how she wondered. What kind of woman had captured Rico's heart and made him as cold and closed-off as he was?

Because that was what she'd discovered over the last two weeks, pleasant as they had been. Rico had no interest in getting to know her, or being known himself. No desire to have a conversation that probed more deeply than the weather or the latest films. There was no need to deepen their relationship now that they were going to be married.

Tonight's party would be his way of introducing her to Roman society as his wife-to-be, and Halina quailed at the thought. She'd only been to one party before, and look how that had turned out. How was she going to be able to manage with everyone's eyes on her, and Rico remaining so solicitous yet so cold?

'Halina?' He knocked on the door of her bedroom. 'The limo is here.'

'All right.' Taking a deep breath, Halina gave her reflection one last inspecting glance. Yesterday Rico had taken her to the prestigious Via dei Condotti to shop in the city's most exclusive boutiques. She'd emerged from the various shops with half a dozen gold-corded bags filled with everything imaginable— lingerie, day dresses, casual clothes, evening gowns.

'I'm not sure what the point of all this is,' she'd told Rico. 'I'm going to start getting bigger soon and nothing will fit.'

He'd merely shrugged. 'You can wear them again after the baby is born. And you have a responsibility to look the part as my wife.'

A remark that had made her want to ask what their marriage was going to look like, what Rico expected from her in all sorts of ways. But she'd held her tongue because she wasn't ready for that conversation. Two weeks of rest had helped her a great deal in recovering both physically and emotionally from the last couple of harrowing months, but she didn't think she had the strength yet to tackle that emotional, explosive subject.

'I'm ready,' she called and, reaching for her gauzy wrap, she turned to the door. She took a deep breath and opened it to find Rico standing there, looking as devastatingly sexy and charismatic in his tuxedo as he had when she'd first laid eyes on him.

'Bella,' Rico murmured, his pupils flaring as his gaze travelled from the top of her head to the tips of her toes. He made no effort to disguise the heat simmering in the silvery depths of his eyes. *'Molta bella.'*

Pleasure coiled within her like a tightly wound spring. She'd taken care with her appearance, styling her hair in a complicated up-do and applying make-up that was both subtle and effective, emphasising her lush mouth and dark eyes. As for the dress…

She'd chosen to wear one Rico hadn't seen during their shopping trip, an emerald-green full-length evening gown with a halter top and a plunging neck-line. It was quite the most daring and sexy thing she'd even worn, and when Rico looked at her with so much unabashed desire she felt heady and powerful. She felt the way she had that fateful night two and a half months ago, and realised afresh how and why it had led her to abandon all common sense.

Rico stretched out one hand and drew her by the fingertips towards the living room and onto the terrace. The night was sultry and warm, the terrace lit only by a sliver of moon and the wash of lights from the buildings spread out before them in a living, breathing map.

'I want to give you this,' Rico said, and withdrew a small black velvet box from the inside pocket of his tuxedo jacket.

Halina's heart stuttered in her chest. 'Is that…?'

'Yes,' he replied as he opened it and showed her its contents. 'It is.'

Halina gazed down at the exquisite solitaire diamond that was big enough to reach to her knuckle. It glittered and sparkled in the darkness, its many facets catching the moonlight. 'It's beautiful,' she whispered. 'And huge.'

'Try it on.'

Wordlessly she held out her hand, unable to keep her fingers from trembling as Rico slid the massive ring onto her finger. It felt heavy, so much so that her hand faltered and Rico caught it up in his own, drawing her even more closely to him.

Their hips nudged and heat flared. This was the closest she'd been to him since the night of the sandstorm, when amidst the fear and uncertainty she'd almost lost her head. Again. Now dizzying sensation spiralled through her, and he was barely touching her.

'Now everyone will know you are mine,' Rico said as he placed his hands on her bare shoulders and drew her even closer towards him. The brush of his lips against her was like an electric shock, twanging all the way through her as he deepened the kiss, turning it into a brand.

Halina swayed as Rico moved his mouth with firm, sure possession over hers, plundering its depths, taking control in this as he did in everything.

He broke the kiss first while stars danced behind her eyes and her knees nearly buckled. Blinking away the haze of desire, she saw his smugly satisfied smile.

'We will have a good marriage, Halina.'

'There's more to a marriage than that,' she returned shakily, and Rico's smile vanished, replaced by a wintry look.

'Not for us.'

She'd known it, of course she had, but it still hurt to have him spell it out so plainly. 'Why not, Rico?'

'What exactly are you asking me?'

'I guess I'm asking you what kind of marriage we will have,' Halina said slowly. Her heart had started beating with painful thuds. 'Because we've never even discussed it.' She held up her hand, heavy with the glittering ring. 'I don't even know when we're getting married.'

'In one month's time.'

'Have you told my father?'

'We'll send him an invitation.'

Halina cringed inwardly at his coolly dismissive tone. Despite the agonising way her father had hurt her, she still missed him and the rest of her family. She hated the thought of them not knowing how she was, or even where she was, but Rico had assured her Sultan Hassan knew she was with him—and that, Rico had said flatly, was all he needed to know.

Now she lowered her hand and gazed down at the ring. 'In one month,' she repeated slowly. 'And what about our marriage? What will it be like?' She hesitated, then dared to ask the question pulsing through her heart. 'I know you don't love me now, but would you ever, perhaps in time?'

She felt Rico stiffen as the seconds ticked on. 'I am not interested in love, Halina. It's an ephemeral emotion. It counts for nothing.'

Pain thudded through her. 'Yet you've said you would love our child.'

'That is different.'

'It's specifically romantic love you're talking about, then?'

A hesitation, telling, painful. 'Yes.'

Halina drew a deep breath. 'So you're telling me you'll never love me?'

'I'm telling you I will provide for you, protect you, seek your happiness above my own. What is love compared to all that?'

She stared at him sorrowfully, unsure of her answer but knowing with a leaden certainty that his wasn't enough.

Rico glanced across at Halina's thoughtful profile, wishing he could see into her mind, even as he acknowledged that he most likely didn't want to know what thoughts lingered there.

He'd planned for the ring—and the kiss—to seal the deal between them and bring her pleasure. What woman didn't like a nice piece of jewellery? And the ring he'd chosen was magnificent. But since the moment he'd slid it onto her finger Halina had cradled her hand as if it was too heavy, as if the ring were a burden or even a wound rather than a symbol of their forthcoming union.

His stomach cramped as he remembered how she'd asked about the nature of their marriage, about whether he would ever come to love her. He'd been postponing such a conversation while Halina regained her strength; her health along with their child's was his main priority. But when asked so directly, he'd had to tell her the truth. He just hoped she could learn to live with it.

'So what is this party for?' she asked as the limo slid through Rome's traffic, the buildings blurring outside the car. She turned to him, looking so achingly lovely he longed to draw her towards him and kiss her lush, plump mouth. He could kiss away all her concerns and worries about the nature of their marriage; he was sure of it. What they would have together in bed would be far better than any tedious notions of love or affection.

He'd waited to reignite their physical relationship because he'd wanted her to feel better physically with her nausea and also because he'd wanted to gain her trust. But now he wondered if kissing away her concerns would be the most expedient option.

'Rico...?' Halina prompted, a frown crinkling her brow. Her eyes still looked sad, just as they had when she'd asked him earlier about their marriage.

'It's a charity event,' he replied. 'For street orphans.'

'Is that a charity you support?'

'Yes.' To the tune of millions of pounds, not that he would tell her as much. It was a charity that cut far too close to the bone, so he kept the amount of his giving secret. Few people knew the nature of his childhood, and no one knew about his father's rejection of him. He did not want to advertise his private shame, or cause people to pity him.

'And what will people there expect of me?' Halina asked, sounding nervous.

'The usual thing at parties. To chat and socialise.' He smiled, wanting to lighten the mood and lift that sadness from her eyes. 'You surely know which fork to use with which course and other such matters?'

'Yes,' Halina allowed. 'But the socialising bit might be beyond me.' Rico looked at her in surprise and she let out a shaky laugh. 'Sometimes I think you have a completely skewed view of my life.'

'Oh?' He frowned, curious and a bit discomfited. He'd assumed, as she was a princess, she'd gone to plenty of parties, dozens of social occasions. 'Enlighten me, then.'

Halina shrugged. 'Before I met you, I'd been to exactly two parties, and they weren't parties the way you probably think of parties. They were diplomatic events at the palace—all I had to do was show up, bow my head and appear modest and subservient. I've never socialised beyond the schoolroom, and before the night I met you I'd never even worn a cocktail dress. This…' she gestured to the gorgeous gown that encased her lush body in a satiny sheath '…is the first evening gown I've ever worn.'

Rico's frown deepened as his wife-to-be surprised him yet again. Yes, he'd known Halina had had a sheltered and even restricted life behind the palace walls, but more and more she showed him just how small it had really been. And he wanted to make it bigger. 'What did you wear to the diplomatic events if not evening gowns?' he asked.

'Traditional dress. Very conservative.'

Something else he hadn't actively considered. 'Is this…these clothes, this lifestyle…difficult for you?'

She laughed, the sound crystalline and musical. 'Difficult? No, definitely not. I love these clothes. I love the freedom of going out to a party.' For a second something sad flickered across her face. 'Believe it or not, I have more freedom here with you in Rome than I did before in Abkar.' *But that's not saying all that much.* Rico could practically see the thought bubble appearing over her head.

'Then I hope you enjoy tonight,' he said sincerely. 'It's your chance to shine.'

And shine she did as they stepped into the elegant ballroom of one of the city's best hotels. Halina was easily the most gorgeous woman in the room, looking like a brilliant green flame in her emerald evening gown. Rico steeled himself not to mind the curious and lustful looks slid her way by just about every male guest. The women looked too, just as intrigued by the woman on his arm. Rico waited until they'd attracted a decent-sized crowd before delivering the bombshell he knew would explode in the entire room.

'Please let me introduce Princess Halina of Abkar,' he said smoothly, his arm linked with Halina's. 'My fiancée.'

Murmurs of shock and surprise rippled through the room as Halina stiffened beside him. Rico pulled her a little closer, determined to stake his claim in every way possible. 'We will be married next month.'

'So soon?' a woman asked with acid sweetness. Rico didn't recognise her, but he certainly knew the tone. He held her gaze, putting iron into his own.

'Yes. Neither of us wish to wait.'

The woman's eyes narrowed and her mouth curved into a speculative smile. Halina put a protective hand over her belly and, from the ensuing ripple of murmurs that spread out through the crowd, Rico knew that just about everyone had seen that revealing action and judged it accurately.

'Let me get you some champagne,' he told Halina, and she gave him a wan smile.

'You mean sparkling water.'

Several people heard, adding fuel to the fires of speculation. Rico knew by the time the evening was at an end everyone there would know Halina was pregnant. Well, so be it. Halina's pregnancy would be physically apparent soon enough, and he would never be ashamed to claim his child.

He asked a waiter for a glass of sparkling water,

then he began to move through the crowd, Halina pressed to his side.

As the hours wound down and the conversation and speculation swirled, Halina became quieter and quieter. At first she'd tried to enter into the various conversations, smiling and nodding, shyly offering her own opinions, but as time passed Rico sensed her withdrawing into herself.

After a five-course meal where they were seated on opposite sides of a table for twelve, she excused herself, disappearing for over twenty minutes before, both impatient and alarmed, Rico went to find her.

He strode down the hotel's opulent corridors, annoyed that he'd been compelled to leave the event to find his errant wife-to-be, even as he fought a growing sense of worry that something was really wrong with her. What if she was ill? What if, God forbid, something had happened to their child?

He asked the attentive staff of the hotel if they'd seen her, and finally tracked her down to the opulent women's powder room down one endless corridor. Not hesitating for a second, Rico rapped on the door.

'Halina? Halina, are you in there?' There was no reply, so he cracked open the door a bit and called again. 'Halina, please answer me if you're in there. Tell me you're all right.'

Two women came to the door, sidling past him with amused glances. 'So attentive,' one of them drawled, and the other gave an unpleasant cackle of laughter. Rico glared at them both.

'Is Princess Halina in the powder room?' he demanded.

One woman, looking spiteful now, shrugged a bony shoulder. 'Why don't you see for yourself?' she called as she walked off with the other woman, their angular bodies and raucous laughter reminding Rico of a pair of glossy, pecking crows.

He pushed open the door to the powder room and strode inside. The place looked empty—a row of gold-plated sinks, a plush settee and several opulent wood-panelled stalls. The room was completely silent, save for the drip of a tap and a sudden, revealing sniff from behind one of the stall doors.

'Halina,' Rico called, his voice rough and urgent. Another sniff sounded. 'Open the door,' he demanded. 'Tell me what's going on.'

After an endless moment Halina unlocked the door and stepped out into the bathroom. Rico gaped at her, taking in her dishevelled hair and tear-stained face, his heart lurching at the sight of her obvious distress.

'Halina,' he said and reached for her. 'What has happened? What's wrong?'

CHAPTER ELEVEN

RICO'S STRONG, WARM hands encased Halina's icy ones as he drew her towards him, his brow furrowed, his expression somewhere between thunderous and terrified.

'Why have you been crying? Has something happened? Is it the baby…?'

'No, it's not the baby.' Halina pulled her hands from his to dash at the tears on her face. She felt embarrassed for falling apart so completely. This evening had been an utter failure, and it was all her fault. She couldn't handle a party. She couldn't handle being Rico's fiancée. 'At least,' she amended, taking a steadying breath, 'it was, in a manner of speaking.'

'What do you mean?' Rico's gaze swept over her, as if looking for open wounds or broken bones. 'Are you hurt?'

Halina let out a shaky laugh, torn between wry amusement and deep, abiding sorrow. 'Yes, Rico,' she managed tartly, 'I am hurt. But you won't find any visible wounds so you can stop looking at me as if you want to take me to the hospital's emergency department.'

'I don't understand.'

'No.' She sighed. 'You wouldn't.' She moved past him to study her reflection. She was even more of a wreck than she'd realised, her supposedly waterproof mascara giving her panda eyes, and her once elegantly styled hair falling about her shoulders in tangled ringlets.

'What is that supposed to mean?' Rico asked, his tone gruff.

Halina sighed and attempted to dab at her mascara even as she recognised a lost cause when she saw one. 'My *feelings* are hurt, Rico,' she said, deciding she needed to speak as plainly as she could. 'Feelings. You know those things you try not to have?'

Rico's mouth thinned. Clearly he didn't appreciate her pathetic attempt at humour. 'Why were your feelings hurt?'

She hesitated, her gaze still on her unhappy reflection. 'It doesn't matter.'

'Yes, it does.' Rico spoke with a force that surprised. 'Who hurt you? Did someone say something, do something? Because if they did it to you, then they did it to me.'

A feeling bloomed in Halina's chest, a mixture of surprise and warmth. It spread through her like sunshine or honey, warming her right down to the tips of her fingers and toes. 'Do you mean that?'

'Of course I do.'

Was that what marriage was? Maybe not love, but something just as fundamental? The question was, could it be enough?

'So what happened, Halina? Tell me.'

'Not here.' She glanced around the bathroom. 'Someone's liable to come in, and I can't cope with another snide remark.'

His frown of concern deepened into a positive scowl. 'So someone did say something to you. One of those women?'

'Not *to* me,' Halina clarified, and felt the tightening of tears in her throat. The snippy, bitchy comments she'd overheard while in the bathroom stall had wounded her deeply, more than she cared to admit to Rico, because even though he wanted to know she knew he wouldn't understand. Not completely.

'Tell me,' he demanded. 'Tell me what they said.'

'Why, so you can punch them?' She let out a hiccupping laugh. 'I will tell you, but can we please go somewhere private?'

'Fine.' He slid his phone out of his pocket and quickly texted a message. 'The limo will meet us out front in five minutes.'

'We're leaving?'

'Do you really want to go back in to the party?'

'No, but I thought you would. This charity is important to you.'

He shrugged. 'Your well-being matters more.'

Which both touched her and made her feel guilty. She really had failed him this evening. Feeling miserable on so many levels, Halina followed Rico out of the bathroom. He took her arm as he strode away from the party so that Halina had to take quick, mincing steps in her tightly fitted evening gown and tottering heels to keep up with him.

'Rico, wait! I can't walk so fast. These shoes are killing me.'

'Sorry.' He glanced at her, contrite. 'I just wanted to get you away from here.'

The limo was waiting for them outside the hotel, and Rico opened the door before ushering Halina inside. She slipped into the luxurious leather interior with a sigh of relief. Every part of her ached.

'Are you in pain?' Rico asked, catching her wince, and Halina managed a laugh.

'No, I'm just not used to these stilettos. They kill my feet.'

'Take them off, then.' Before she could do so he reached down, undid the straps of her shoes and slipped them off her feet. Halina let out a gusty sigh of relief, then gave a little gasp of surprise when Rico took her feet and drew them up to his lap. When his thumbs began to massage powerful circles on their soles she wriggled with pleasure and couldn't keep a moan of delight from escaping her.

'Oh, my goodness, that feels fantastic.'

Rico laughed softly. 'I can tell.'

He reached over and tucked one of the throw pillows adorning the limo's seats behind her head. 'There. Now tell me what happened at the party.'

Halina's eyes fluttered closed as she surrendered to Rico's tender ministrations, his fingers continuing to work their magic on her aching feet. 'It wasn't such a big deal. I'm sorry I made it so.'

'That's for me to say, not you. What happened, Halina?'

She sighed and then wriggled again with pleasure as Rico's hands moved up to her ankles, his thumbs tracing the delicate bones.

'I was in one of the bathroom stalls and some women came in. They started talking about me—and you.'

His fingers stilled for only a second before he continued with the slow, rhythmic circles. 'And what did they say?'

'They knew I was pregnant. I don't know how...'

'You put your hand on your belly during our engagement announcement and then you asked for sparkling water.'

'Oh.' Now she felt stupid. 'Well, that explains it, then,' she said with an attempt at a laugh.

'I don't mind people knowing, Halina,' Rico said, his voice low and sure. 'I will never mind. You're going to be my wife and you're carrying my child.'

'Are you sorry?' Halina blurted, opening her eyes. In the darkness of the car she couldn't make out his expression.

'Sorry...?'

'That you slept with me. That I became pregnant. That I...that I ruined your life.'

'Halina.' Rico leaned forward so his gaze met hers and she could see how fiercely his silvery eyes glittered. 'You have not ruined my life.'

'But to be suddenly burdened with a wife and baby you didn't want… And you had all those mistresses…' A sudden, horrible thought occurred to her, one that now seemed appallingly obvious. 'Are you…are you going to keep on with them…after we marry?'

'What?' Rico's brows drew together in a ferocious frown. 'Of course not. Do you honestly think I would?'

'You didn't ask for this, Rico.'

'Neither did you. And, in any case, I believe I will be wholly satisfied in that department by my wife.' His hand slid from her ankle to her knee, his fingers splayed across her tender skin as his gaze remained hot and intent on hers. 'Perhaps I should remind you how good we are together, *bella*. How explosive.'

Halina's breath came out in a shuddery rush and the sensitive skin of her knee tingled. His fingers felt warm and very sure as they started to slide upwards. 'You've barely touched me in two weeks,' she whispered. 'Not since you saw me again.'

'I wanted you to rest.' His smile turned wolfish, his eyes filled with heat. 'To regain your strength.'

'Plus I looked like a worn-out dishrag.'

'You have always been beautiful to me. Never doubt that.' With his gaze still fastened on hers, he moved his hand to her inner thigh, his warm palm sliding upwards in a sure, fluid movement. Halina shuddered, every nerve on over-sensitised alert as his fingers skimmed along her skin.

'We're so good together, Halina,' Rico murmured as he continued to stroke her thigh. 'We always have been.'

'You mean the one time.'

'I am looking forward to many others. You have ruined me for other women.'

'That's what someone said about you.' Her breath came out in jerks and bursts as his fingers crept even closer to her feminine centre. If he touched her there, she thought she might melt—or explode.

'What do you mean?' One finger skimmed the lace of her underwear, making her shudder. Halina slid a little lower down on the seat.

'In the bathroom…that first night…some super-model you'd slept with… The women said she'd been ruined for life by you, because you're so…' His fingers were becoming more insistent, more daring, sliding beneath her underwear, skimming her tantalised flesh and then going even deeper, with sure, knowing strokes. Pleasure swirled inside her, obscuring her senses so she could barely think, much less speak. 'They said…they said you were so good,' she half-moaned as her body arched upwards. 'At sex.' With a little cry she gave herself up to the pleasure crashing over her and felt herself go liquid and boneless.

As the last shudders of her climax rippled through her, Rico leaned over and pressed a hard kiss to her mouth. 'Which I've just proved, I think.'

She opened her eyes, dazed and more than a little embarrassed to be slouched on the seat, her elegant gown rucked up halfway to her hips, her wanton pleasure so very evident.

She struggled up to sitting, pushing her hair out of her face. 'I must look a mess,' she muttered.

'You look beautiful.' Rico touched her chin with his fingertips. 'Do you know how enflaming it is to see you come apart under my touch? Do you know what it does to me?' Wordlessly Halina shook her head, shocked by the admission, by the blatant need she saw in his eyes and felt in the tautness of his body. 'When we get back to the apartment,' Rico said, his voice roughening, 'I'll show you.'

Desire thrummed through Rico, a slow burn that threatened to ignite into a full conflagration. Seeing Halina respond to his touch, her face and body both suffused with pleasure, had been a severe test of his self-control. He'd wanted to take her right there on the seat of his limo, in the kind of helpless display of overwhelming need that he never gave into.

So he didn't. He wanted her—heaven help them both how much he did—but he still clung to his self-control, if only by his fingertips.

The limo pulled up to his building and without a word Rico emerged from the back, holding Halina's hand as he drew her along.

'My shoes,' she protested, and he saw she was barefoot.

'They don't matter. Forget them.' His self-control only extended so far.

With a little laugh Halina did, following him into the darkened foyer of the building and then into the lift. That was how far his self-control went; as soon as the doors closed, he pulled her into his arms, plundering her mouth as he backed her up against the wall.

She gasped, driving her hands through his hair as she surrendered to his touch, wrapping her arms around him and pulling him even closer.

It still wasn't enough. He yanked her dress up to her waist, needing to feel her against him.

'Rico…' His name was a soft protest and he stilled, shocked by his own urgent actions.

'Do you want me?' he demanded, unable to keep from saying the words. Voicing his fear. 'Do you want me as much as I want you?'

'You know I do.'

The doors to his apartment opened and with a sound nearing a growl Rico swept Halina up into his arms and strode to his bedroom. 'Then show me.'

'I already have,' she protested breathlessly as he peeled her dress off her and laid her on the bed. 'How could you doubt it, Rico? I've been putty in your hands since the moment I first laid eyes on you.'

'Good.' He pulled off his tie and tuxedo shirt, studs flying everywhere and clattering to the floor. 'That's how I want it to be.'

The self-control he'd been so determined, so *des-*

perate to hold onto was in shreds. All he could think of, all he could feel, was his need for her. Shucking off the rest of his clothes, Rico pulled Halina into his arms. The feel of her golden, silken skin against his was an exquisite torture.

'I've been dreaming of this,' he muttered against her skin, wanting to touch and taste her all at once. 'Dreaming of this ever since you walked out of my hotel suite all those weeks ago.'

'So have I,' Halina whispered, her body arching under his touch. 'Even if I tried to keep myself from it.'

Just as he had, because such need was weakness. But now he didn't care. Now he simply wanted—and took.

When he slid inside her velvety depths he felt a crashing sense of relief, almost as if a burden had been lifted. This felt right and true, the home he'd never had. Then she arched up to meet him, matching his thrusts, and he stopped thinking at all.

Later, when his heart rate had started to slow and he felt himself come back to his senses, Rico reviewed his actions as dispassionately as he could. Yes, he'd lost control. Completely. But so had Halina. The fact was they shared an incredible chemistry, and that was no bad thing. So as long as he kept the loss of control in the realm of the bedroom, he would be satisfied. He wouldn't be in danger of losing anything to Halina…such as the heart he'd always acted as if he didn't have.

Next to him Halina stirred sleepily. 'That was a nice way to end the evening.'

'Perhaps the evening is just beginning.' Rico rolled over to face her. 'But we never finished our conversation. What did those women say?'

'It really doesn't matter...'

He hated the thought of her being hurt. 'I think it does.'

With a sigh Halina rolled onto her back. 'They just said they couldn't believe you'd finally been snared—that was the word I think they used. And the fact that I was pregnant and a princess could be the only reason you'd ever marry me, because you were obviously way out of my league.'

Rico stiffened, a new fury starting to boil through him. How dared those insipid, catty women say such things about his chosen bride?

'I don't know why you seem angry,' Halina remarked lightly as she rolled back to face him. 'It's all true.'

'What? No, it isn't.'

'Come on, Rico.' Despite her light tone, pain flashed in her eyes. 'Let's be honest. I know there are a lot of things we can't have in our marriage, but surely truth isn't one of them?'

'It's not true,' he insisted stubbornly.

'It is,' Halina returned, her tone just as stubborn. 'You know it is. You never would have married me if I hadn't been pregnant, and the fact that I'm royal no doubt has something to do with it too.'

'What are you saying? That if you'd been a nobody I wouldn't have married you?'

'Would you have?'

'I would always,' Rico said flatly, fighting back a tidal wave of fury, 'marry the mother of my child.'

'So I guess you didn't get a woman pregnant before.'

'No, I always took precautions, for a reason.'

She nodded slowly. 'And I'd told you it was safe. I'm sorry.'

He shook his head, annoyed and exasperated by the whole conversation. He didn't want to tread over this old ground yet again. He didn't want to be reminded of how he used to be, either. He was different now—just not *that* different.

'My point,' Halina said after a moment, 'Is that my pregnancy is what precipitated your proposal. How's that for an alliteration?' She gave him a teasing smile but Rico didn't have it in him to respond in kind.

His fury was fading, replaced by a far more alarming confusion as he realised that Halina was right, at least in part. He never would have married her if she hadn't been pregnant. He never even would have seen her again. It was blindingly obvious, but it didn't sit well with him. At all.

'I should go back to my own bed,' Halina said, starting to rise. Rico stayed her with one hand.

'You'll sleep here.'

Even in the darkness of the room he saw the surprise flash across her face. 'I thought you never slept with a woman—'

'You're going to be my wife,' Rico interjected fiercely. 'And we'll sleep together from now on. It's time,' he added, drawing her towards him so she was nestled snugly against his chest, 'That we started to plan the wedding.'

CHAPTER TWELVE

'THIS DRESS IS very discreet.' The sales assistant gave Halina a knowing smile as she gestured to a gorgeous dress of ivory satin with a convenient empire waist to hide Halina's small but growing bump. She was fifteen weeks pregnant and only just starting to show.

It had been three weeks since she and Rico had reconsummated their relationship, three weeks of virtually living as man and wife, even if they weren't going to say the vows for another fortnight. Three happy, hopeful yet so uncertain weeks, and with every passing day Halina felt more and more anxious.

She had spent every night in Rico's bed, as well as in his arms. He was a tender and attentive lover, awakening her body to sensations and desires she'd never experienced before.

As she'd grown in experience, she had also grown in confidence, daring to touch and explore his body as he did hers. It had brought an intense intimacy that left Halina breathless with longing for Rico to feel the same as she did…even as she forced herself to acknowledge that he didn't, he couldn't, not when he'd gone through a woman a week for most of his adult life. Sex was just a physical exercise for him, not the emotional, soul-shattering experience it had become for her.

As for out of bed… Rico was attentive then, too. Solicitous to her every need and comfort—often coming home with some treat she'd been craving, accompanying her to her doctor appointments and helping with the planning of their wedding which, according to the city's tabloids and gossip magazines, was going to be the event of the year.

Halina wasn't sure how she felt about that; in the weeks since that first, awful party they'd gone out on several social occasions and she'd managed to hold her head up high, despite several women's sneering looks and whispering comments.

'They're just jealous,' Rico said blandly, and Halina had laughed.

'That's a rather arrogant comment, you know.'

'But it's true.' And she knew it was.

As the wedding loomed closer, she veered between excitement and a growing terror. Excitement because part of her was looking forward to being part of a family again, to starting a new life with Rico. She'd enjoyed these last few weeks with him, more than she'd ever expected to, but the terror came from the creeping fear that it wasn't enough and it never would be.

His care, his solicitude, his thorough attentiveness in bed—none of it would be enough, because he didn't love her. He'd made that very clear in a thousand painful ways. He would never love her, and she had to accept that, learn to live with it, because she had no choice. As much freedom as she felt she had now, she still lived under the worst restriction of all.

'Would you like to try it on?' the assistant asked, and Halina nodded, needing a distraction from her circling and increasingly unhappy thoughts. She also needed a wedding dress; the church and reception hall had been booked, the meal planned, the champagne ordered and the guests, all six hundred of them, invited. Although she'd been looking for a while, she hadn't yet found a dress she liked—and it was getting late.

Halina went into the dressing room and slipped into the empire-waist dress. The bodice shimmered with crystal jet and diamanté, and the skirt fell in a drop of exquisite ivory satin, swirling around her ankles. It was simple and elegant and, as the assistant said, very discreet.

Halina tried to picture herself walking down the aisle in the huge church and inwardly trembled. She'd be walking alone; her father had refused to attend the wedding, or let her mother or sisters attend. Their absence made her relationship with Rico feel even lonelier and more lacking. He was all she had in the world, and he didn't love her.

'What does *signorina* think?' the assistant called, and Halina gazed at her pale face, her wide dark eyes.

'It's fine,' she called back tonelessly. 'Perfect. I'll take it.'

Her fingers shook as she fumbled with the hook-and-eye fasteners at the back of the dress. What was wrong with her? She'd been happy these last three weeks; she really had. There had been so much to enjoy, and yet…

Marriage. A loveless marriage. For ever. She closed her eyes and leaned her forehead against the cool mirror. Why did it matter so much? Why did it make her ache so?

'Signorina?' The assistant peeked through the curtain and Halina jerked back, embarrassed to be caught looking as if she were about to fall apart.

'I'll be straight out.'

The woman smiled sympathetically. 'Everyone gets cold feet, no? It is normal.'

It wasn't her cold feet she was worried about but Rico's icy heart. Quickly she slipped out of the dress and handed it to the assistant. 'Thank you.'

'You are sure…?'

'Yes.' She was sure about the dress, if nothing else at this moment.

Halina dressed quickly, as Rico was planning to meet her for lunch at a new upscale restaurant off the Via dei Condotti and she didn't want him sensing that she was worried or upset. He would just harangue her, demanding to know what was wrong and how he could fix it. Touching at times, but he couldn't fix this. He wouldn't want to.

'Did you find a dress?' Rico asked when she walked into the restaurant fifteen minutes later. He stood up as she came to the table and kissed her cheek.

'Yes, I have found one.' Halina sat down and smiled. 'I think it's very pretty.'

Rico scanned her face, a slight frown settling between his brows. 'What's wrong?'

He was so irritatingly perceptive, Halina reflected. A strange quality for man who claimed to have no use for feelings. 'Nothing's wrong,' she said and picked up her menu. Now that thankfully her nausea had gone, she found she was ravenous.

'Something's wrong, Halina. I can tell.'

Halina looked up from the menu, her eyebrows raised. 'How can you tell?'

Rico shrugged, seeming slightly discomfited by the question. 'I just can. There's something about you…it's like a sixth sense, I suppose. We're attuned to each other.'

Which could have been heartening, but wasn't. She didn't want to be *attuned*. She wanted to be loved. The realisation solidified inside her, although she'd been trying to talk herself out of it for weeks. Why did she care if Rico loved her or not, when he promised her so much else?

The answer came suddenly in a tidal wave of amazement and despair.

She loved him. She'd gone and fallen in love with him, even though she'd known it was foolish, the stupidest thing she could ever do. Yet she'd still done it.

Her heart hadn't been able to resist because Rico was gentle, kind and fiercely protective, because he made her laugh and ache and sing.

This was love, then, that ephemeral emotion Rico dismissed out of hand. And it was so much more than that, because Halina knew what it meant. It meant she would love him no matter what; it meant she would love him even if he didn't love her back.

She'd wondered what love felt like, if she'd really know when it was missing or whether she'd found it, and now here was her proof. She loved Rico, and it filled her with both joy and despair because she knew, no matter what she felt, that he utterly refused to love her back.

'Well?' Rico demanded. 'Has something happened? Has someone said something? Tell me.'

'I don't want to, Rico,' Halina said wearily. She knew he wouldn't let it drop, just as she knew he'd hate to hear what was really troubling her—the realisation that thudded through her, a wonder and fear.

Rico's frown deepened. 'Why don't you want to?'

'Because there's no point, and it will just annoy you.' As much as it hurt her to say it. 'You don't have to be such a bull dog about everything, you know? I'm allowed to have some thoughts I can keep to myself.' Because it would horrify him to know she'd fallen in love with him. That much she knew.

'I'm hardly asking you to tell me your every thought,' Rico protested. 'But, if something is troubling you, I want to fix it.'

'Trust me, you can't fix this.'

That, of course, did nothing to appease him. 'There must be something I can do,' Rico insisted, and Halina almost smiled. Her husband-to-be hated the thought that he was not all-powerful.

'There isn't,' she informed him firmly. 'Shall we order?'

Rico looked unconvinced but he beckoned the hovering waiter over and they ordered their meals.

'You are happy with the dress?' Rico asked once the waiter had left them alone.

'Yes, it's very nice.' Although now she could barely remember what it looked like. It wasn't the way she had wanted to buy her wedding dress, alone and anonymous in a boutique. If she'd been at home, her sisters would have surrounded her, jabbering excitedly, and her mother would have been there to offer benevolent and wise advice. Even her father would have wanted to see the dress, and offer an opinion.

Sudden tears stung her eyes and she blinked them back rapidly, but not before Rico noticed.

'Halina,' he said, his voice low and urgent as he leaned forward. 'You must tell me what is wrong. I can't stand to see you so obviously unhappy.'

'I just miss my family,' Halina said, which was the truth, if not all of it. 'I wish they could be here for the wedding.'

Rico sat back, his lips pressed together. 'You are right, in that there is nothing I can do about that.'

'I know.' She sniffed and took a sip of sparkling

water. 'I'm sorry. I'll be better in a moment.' She managed a wobbly smile. 'It's all these pregnancy hormones making me emotional.' But it was so much more.

'You don't need to be sorry.' Rico was subjecting her to one of his thorough, considering glances. 'But there's something else, isn't there?'

'Oh, Rico.' Halina let out a shuddery laugh as she rolled her eyes. 'What if there was?'

'Then I want to know.'

She stared at him for a moment, knowing he wouldn't let it go. Well, fine. She'd asked for honesty from him once; now he could have it from her, at least some of it.

'All right.' She took a deep, steadying breath. 'The truth is, I'm sad because I know you don't love me, and from what you've said you'll probably never love me. I'm trying to come to terms with it, but it's hard. I know I was willing to marry a virtual stranger, but a cold, loveless union is not what I've ever wanted for my life.'

Rico stared at Halina, trying not to let his emotions show on his face. His utter horror at what she'd just stated with such stark, bleak honesty. He must not have done a very good job because Halina let out a huff of humourless laughter.

'You don't have to look quite so appalled. Consider the bright side—I do know what I'm getting into.' She looked away, blinking rapidly, appalling him further. 'You made sure of that.'

'Yes, but I… I didn't realise you wanted…love quite so much.'

'Is it so surprising? Isn't it what most people want?' She turned back to give him a direct, challenging look. 'Perhaps you're the strange one, Rico, not me.'

'Perhaps.' He knew, on some level, she'd wanted love. She'd said as much, but he'd been sure he could convince her otherwise.

What *was* love anyway? Nothing more than a feeling, as ephemeral as the morning mist. Halina could learn to live without it, just as he had. Everything would be better that way. Happier, even. He just had to convince her of it.

Rico eyed her carefully. 'Halina,' he began, choosing each word with delicate precision, 'Just because we do not love each other…we can still be happy together.'

'Can we?' Tears shimmered in her eyes and she blinked them back resolutely. 'I know all this emotion is appalling you, Rico. I'm sorry.'

'For heaven's sake, you don't need to be sorry.' Did she think he was that intransigent, that hard and unyielding? Perhaps once he had been, but now… He *had* changed, at least a little. Just not too much. 'You can't help the way you feel.'

'Just as you can't help the way you don't.' She forced a smile. 'So there we are.'

'It doesn't have to be all gloom and despair,' Rico persisted, trying to keep the impatience and urgency from his voice. 'What is love anyway, Halina? A feeling? A warm glow in your heart?'

She flinched at the scorn he'd unintentionally and instinctively put into those words. 'Maybe that's a sign of it, Rico, but it's not all love is.' Her lip curled, and now she was as contemptuous as he was. 'Love is so much more than that, which you should know, since you've loved someone before.'

He felt himself go still. 'What makes you say that?'

'You said it before,' she answered with a shrug, her pain-filled gaze sliding away from his. 'You told me it was a long time ago, but she obviously hurt you very badly if you can't bear the thought of letting yourself love someone years later.'

'She?' Rico repeated blankly, and Halina turned back to him with a frown.

'The woman, whoever she was.'

'There was no woman, Halina.' Perhaps it would have been easier, safer, to pretend there had been, but it didn't feel fair to Halina and he didn't want her to labour under the misapprehension that he'd loved another woman but wouldn't love her. 'I told you before, I've never been in love with anyone.'

'Then who was it who broke your heart?' Halina asked in a whisper. Rico flinched at the phrase.

Broke his heart. So trite, so real. 'It was my father,' he said after a tense pause. 'He hurt me very badly when I was a child and I never forgot it.'

'What did he do?'

'He didn't love me back,' Rico said simply. Even

that felt like admitting way too much. Halina stared at him, her gaze both searching and yearning.

'And that's why you don't want to love anyone? Because of something that happened when you were a child?'

'It taught me a valuable lesson,' Rico said shortly.

'Which was?'

'That love isn't real. Whether it's a warm glow or not, that doesn't matter. It doesn't last. It doesn't change things, and you can't count on it or trust it. Frankly, we're both better off without it, Halina.'

'Of course you would think that.'

'Yes, I would,' Rico returned, his voice gaining force. He felt a deep-seated need, bordering on a compulsion, to prove this to her. To liberate her from such childish notions, as well as cement the foundation of their own future happiness. 'Think about it, Halina. You want me to love you. What does that even mean? What would it look like, practically?'

She flushed, looking as if she resented the question. 'If I have to spell it out to you...'

He reached across the table to cover her hand with his own. 'Humour me. Please.'

'Fine.' She pulled her hand away and folded her arms. 'It would mean I was the most important thing to you. That you couldn't bear to be away from me. That I made the sun shine more brightly and the sky look more blue. That I complete you.' She shook her head. 'How many clichés do I have to pull out of the book, Rico? Love just *is*. Either you love someone or you don't, and if you don't, then whatever you feel—whether it's affection or duty or something in between—is eventually going to fade and pale. At some point in the future it's not going to be enough, and that's what I don't want to have happen. I don't want to look up from my dinner or roll over in bed and see that knowledge in your eyes.'

'I swear to you,' Rico said in a low voice that thrummed with sincerity, 'that would never happen.'

'You can't make that promise.'

He put his hands flat on the table, a sudden fury coursing through him. 'And you think love is the failsafe guarantee, Halina? That, if I loved you, that feeling would never fade? Because, I can assure you, it would. Love is a guarantee of absolutely nothing. Haven't you learned that yourself? Look at your own father. You thought he loved you but he would have killed your own baby if he could have, and now he won't even come to your wedding. Is that love?'

Her face crumpled and he regretted his harsh words. He'd been so caught up in the moment, in his own memories. He reached for her hands. 'Halina…'

'Maybe you're right, Rico,' Halina said, her expression composed now, although her voice trembled. 'Love can fade, or at least seem as if it does. But I choose to believe, and to hope. People make mistakes, they do unloving things, but at the core of their being the love remains. And I choose to believe that my father still loves me, and eventually he'll realise the mistakes he made. *That's* the difference. Someone who loves you can still let you down. They're only human. But because you love them, and they love you, you keep going. You forgive and you grow stronger, and you move on. Together. You asked me what love is. Well, that's my definition.'

Rico stared at her, humbled by her brave honesty and also by the gaping emptiness he felt in himself. Had he ever felt that, either to give or to receive? Did he even know what love was?

'So we're right back at the beginning,' Halina said with an attempt at a laugh. She shook her head sadly. 'There's no solution, is there, Rico? We're going to get married, but you will never love me. I just have to live with it.'

'I might not love you,' Rico said, 'but, as I told you before, I will protect and provide for you. Always. I will be loyal and faithful, and I will do anything in my power to make you happy. Isn't that enough?'

Her mouth curved in a sorrowful smile as she answered. 'I suppose it will have to be.'

CHAPTER THIRTEEN

A WEEK BEFORE the wedding Halina woke up in the middle of the night with terrible stomach cramps. It had been a week since her all-too-honest conversation with Rico, a week of learning to live without love and finding a way to be happy. At times she'd felt she was on the verge of finding it: when she and Rico could laugh together, when he reached for her in bed. But then memories would rush through her, or he would roll away, and she feared she'd always be searching for that ever-elusive feeling.

Now she lay in bed, blinking up at the ceiling as her stomach cramped, muscles contracting painfully. She was only four months along, and in the last few days she'd felt the first flutters of movement, which had filled her with joy. Now she feared something was wrong.

Quietly she slid from the bed and went to the bathroom, hoping that the issue was merely a spicy meal that had disagreed with her. But when she saw the rusty streak of blood on the toilet paper she knew otherwise.

Her soft scream had Rico bolting upright in bed. 'Halina?'

She came out of the bathroom, her whole body trembling. 'I'm bleeding,' she whispered. Her body throbbed with terror as her stomach continued to cramp. 'Rico, I'm bleeding.'

Rico's eyes widened as he got her full meaning. 'I'll take you to the hospital,' he said, already getting out of bed. 'To the emergency department, right now.'

Halina watched, fear hammering through her, as Rico pulled on a shirt and trousers. He was in the middle of buttoning his shirt when he saw that she hadn't moved from the doorway of the bathroom.

'Halina, we need to go.'

'I'm scared.' The two words fell softly into the stillness. She wrapped her arms around herself. 'I don't want to lose this baby. I can't. Not after everything…'

'You won't.' Rico took her by the shoulders and stared into her eyes, his expression both grim and comforting. 'You won't. The doctors will figure out what's going on. They'll help you and they will help our baby.'

She nodded, wanting to believe him, needing to. Her teeth chattered; she felt icy cold.

'Come on,' Rico said gently, steering her towards the bureau. 'Let's get you dressed.' Halina felt like a child as she stood there and let Rico tenderly strip her nightgown from her body. He found one of her new maternity tops and loose trousers and helped her shrug them on.

'I'm sorry,' she choked. 'I feel frozen…'

'Shh.' Rico brushed a kiss against her forehead. 'It's all right…it's going to be all right.'

He took her hand and together they walked out to his car, a luxury sports model that he used in his down time with a private parking space. Halina slid into the passenger seat and wrapped her arms around herself. Even though it was a balmy evening at the very end of September, she felt so very cold.

The emergency department of the local hospital was brightly lit and bustling despite the late hour. Several rows of hard plastic seats were filled with people with various ailments and injuries. Rico strode to the front to talk to the triage nurse while Halina sank into a seat, desperately trying to hold onto her composure as well as her hope. Her stomach still cramped, off and on, off and on.

Rico strode back to her then sat down next to her and took her hand. 'You're freezing,' he said, and chafed her hand between his own. Halina gave him a shaky smile.

'I feel like I'll never get warm. Maybe it's shock.'

'It's going to be okay, Halina.'

'I know you want that to be the case, but it might not be.' Her voice wobbled. 'It might not be. This isn't in your control, Rico, just like the sandstorm. I know you hate that, but it's true.'

'I do hate it.' Rico's voice was low and fierce. 'I hate it absolutely.' His hands squeezed hers. 'But I also believe it's going to be okay. It has to be.'

Looking at the agony written in harsh lines on his features, Halina knew he meant that with every fibre of his being. Rico couldn't take this not being okay. She couldn't cope with it, just as he couldn't, and it made her cling to him all the more.

'Signora Falcone?'

Halina gave Rico a startled glance as she heard the nurse call out her soon-to-be name.

'It seemed easier,' he muttered, and rose from the seat before helping her to her feet. 'We're here,' he called to the nurse.

Halina focused on staying calm as she followed the nurse to a cubicle in the hospital's busy emergency department. After a short wait a doctor bustled in, smiling in a slightly distracted way.

'What seems to be the problem?' she asked as he soaped her hands at the little sink.

Haltingly, Halina explained about the cramps and bleeding. The doctor frowned as he dried his hands.

'You're about sixteen weeks along?'

'Yes, just sixteen weeks.'

'It can be normal to have a little bleed during your pregnancy, but it can also be a sign of something wrong. Why don't we have a listen for the heartbeat?'

Halina nodded and lay back on the examining table, her mouth dry, her heart thudding. Rico stood by her, his hand still encasing hers.

The doctor turned on the Doppler and began to press Halina's belly, looking for the heartbeat. All they heard was the whoosh of her own body and blood, not the lovely, galloping sound of their baby's heart.

Halina closed her eyes, willing to hear that wonderful sound. This couldn't be the end. It just couldn't be. *Please, baby*, she prayed silently. *Please live.*

The doctor switched off the Doppler, looking serious. Halina risked a glance at Rico and saw his jaw was clenched tightly, his eyes dark and focused.

'I'll send you to the ultrasound department for a scan,' the doctor said. 'Sometimes it can be difficult to find the heartbeat.' He gave them both a sympathetic smile. 'But of course, it could also be that something has gone wrong. We'll only know when we see the scan.'

Halina nodded. She felt icy and numb now, too numb to be afraid any more. She'd feared the worst already, and it seemed likely. Wordlessly she pulled her top down and she and Rico went back to the waiting room to wait until she was called for a scan.

Neither of them spoke as they sat in the brightly lit room while people bustled and moved around them— children sleeping on mother's laps, babies crying. Halina looked away from the tear-filled eyes of a chubby-cheeked cherub. What she wouldn't give to have a baby in her arms right now, even one that was crying and in pain.

'It's going to be okay,' Rico said in a low voice, and Halina turned to him with a sudden, surprising spurt of fury.

'Stop saying that,' she returned, her voice just as

low. 'You don't know. You can't know. And at the moment, Rico, it looks like things aren't going to be all right. The doctor couldn't even find a heartbeat—' She broke off with a shuddering breath and looked away.

'You're right,' Rico answered after a moment. 'I don't know, and I hate that, because I don't know what to do, Halina. I want to help you and I can't.'

Tears stung her eyes and she blinked them back. 'You can help me by just walking with me through this, whatever happens,' she said steadily. 'Don't try to fix it or control it, Rico—just be with me. That's what I want.' She turned to him, blinking back more tears that threatened to fall. 'Can you do that?'

He looked at her seriously, his mouth a firm line, an agony in his eyes. 'Yes,' he said. 'I can do that.'

He hated everything about this. He hated watching Halina's fear and pain, feeling it himself, twice the agony. He hated having their carefully constructed world break apart, shatter into pieces. He thought of the baby nestled in Halina's womb and willed it to live. He hadn't realised just how much he wanted this child until it was at risk. Until everything he'd shared and built with Halina was at risk.

The knowledge jolted him, like missing the last stair. This wasn't just about their baby; it was about him and Halina. Their relationship. Their marriage. Over the last few weeks he'd got used to having Halina with him; he enjoyed it, counted on it, even. And he wasn't willing to give that up.

But if their baby had died…there was no reason to get married. No reason at all, and with an uncomfortable, prickling sensation Rico realised that Halina would no doubt be glad to get away from him. She'd made it clear several weeks ago—hell, all along—that she was willing to marry him but she didn't actually want to…because she wanted someone who would love her. Who could love her.

And he couldn't.

'Signora Falcone?'

Halina looked up, her face pale, her lips set in a firm line. Rico reached for her hand and together they walked towards the nurse, braced for the worst.

The ultrasound room was dim and quiet as Halina lay back once again on the examining table and the technician squirted cold, clear gel on her bare belly, her baby bump barely visible. She looked so vulnerable lying there, waiting, worrying, and Rico's heart ached for her. Ached for them, because he was so afraid it was all slipping away.

He knew that fear. He knew it far too well, because he remembered feeling it when his father had dropped him off on the steps of the orphanage in Salerno, his face grim but determined.

'They'll take care of you here,' he'd said while Rico had fought tears as he'd begged for his father to keep him. Not to leave him. He'd cried like a baby; he'd clung to his father's sleeve and his father had had to push him off.

Then he'd watched his father walk away; he hadn't

looked back once. And in that moment Rico had resolved never to let someone hurt him like that again.

'Rico, look.' Halina grabbed his sleeve, just as he had with his father, and he blinked back the memories as he was startled into the present. 'Look, Rico. Our baby!'

He focused on the ultrasound screen, and the beautiful sight of their tiny baby wriggling around like a jumping bean.

'Baby looks fine,' the technician said with a smile, and Halina let out an incredulous, shuddery laugh of joy. Rico's smile nearly split his face. 'It looks, Signora Falcone,' the technician continued, 'as if you've had a sub-chorionic haematoma.'

'A what?' Halina asked, her voice filled with nervousness.

The technician gave her a quick, reassuring smile. 'Basically a bleed between your baby and the uterine wall.'

'Is it dangerous?' Rico asked, his voice harsher than he'd meant it to be.

'It doesn't have to be.' The technician gave them both a sympathetic smile. 'Of course, any bleeding in pregnancy can be a cause of concern, and a haematoma of this size is definitely something we need to keep an eye on.'

None of which sounded particularly good. 'So what now?' Rico asked. 'What do we do?'

'Signora Falcone can continue as normal,' the technician said. 'Which is what we'd advise. But we'd also advise slowing down a little if possible—not being on your feet too much, or carrying anything heavy, that sort of thing.' She smiled at Halina. 'Giving both you and your baby the best chance possible. And, if you have any more bleeding, don't hesitate to call.'

Rico's mind was still spinning as they drove back home, dawn lighting the empty streets of Rome and touching them with rosy gold.

Back in the penthouse Halina went straight to bed, and Rico tucked her in as if she were a child. 'See?' he said as he brushed a kiss across her lips. 'I told you it was going to be okay.'

Halina gave him a wan smile; she looked utterly exhausted. Within moments she was asleep.

Back in the living area Rico pulled his laptop towards him and spent several hours finding out everything he could about sub-chorionic haematomas. The information was mixed, with some specialists saying they heightened the chance of miscarriage, and others saying they had no effect.

His eyes gritty and aching, Rico stared out at the city and vowed to do everything he could to keep Halina and their baby safe. They'd come so close today to losing it all and it had scared him.

It had scared him even more how devastated he'd been at the thought of not losing just his child, but Halina too. He was starting to care for her and that prospect terrified him more than anything.

How could he make Halina happy, love their baby and yet keep the emotional distance from her he knew he needed? The lines were blurring more and more every day. Soon it would be impossible…and what then?

'What time is it?'

Rico looked up, startled out of his thoughts, to see Halina standing in the doorway, her hair in a dark cloud about her face, her expression still sleepy.

'I don't know.' He checked his watch. 'About ten in the morning. You should get back in bed.'

'I can't spend the next five months in bed, Rico.'

'You heard what the technician said.'

'Yes, I did. Did you?' With a wry smile she crossed the room and curled up on the opposite end of the sofa. 'She said I needed to take it a bit easier, not that I needed to be bedridden.'

'Still…'

She turned to him, her smile gone, her expression serious. 'Don't you think I'm going to do everything in my power to take care of this baby?'

Slightly abashed, Rico nodded. Yes, he believed that. Of course he did.

Halina drew her knees up, resting her chin on top. 'Still, it could all go wrong,' she said quietly. 'We have to be prepared for that.'

'Just as we have to do everything we can to make sure that doesn't happen,' Rico returned. 'I'm going to call off the wedding.'

'What?' She turned to him, startled, her eyes wide and dark.

'It's too much strain and pressure on you. We can

have a quiet wedding later, or reschedule a big ceremony, if that's what you prefer.'

'But all the preparations…all the money you spent…'

'What does money matter? Your health is more important. Our child's health. Besides, perhaps if we wait a while your father will come round and decide to attend.'

Pain flashed across her face and she nodded slowly. 'Yes. Maybe.' She sounded so sad that Rico ached to hold her, but he didn't, because something about Halina right now was cool and brittle, as if she were trying to maintain a certain distance. Her next words confirmed it.

'But Rico…if I do lose this baby…we need to talk about that.'

He tensed, his jaw clenched. 'Let's not court disaster, Halina.'

'Let's also be prepared,' she returned evenly. 'Isn't that your motto? Wasn't that why you had all those provisions in the car when we were trapped in the sandstorm in the desert? Because you like to be prepared.'

'Yes, but—'

'So let's be prepared for this,' Halina said steadily. 'If I lose the baby, we don't have to marry. You're free.'

Why did he now hate that thought? 'And what about you?' he asked. 'Are you free?'

'Yes,' Halina returned after a pause. 'Yes, I will

be. I told you before, I never wanted a marriage without love.'

He fought to keep his expression neutral when everything in him wanted to cry out, to resist and deny. 'So what will you do, in this worst-case scenario? Return to Abkar?'

She let out a small huff of sad laughter and shrugged. 'Maybe I'll get that apartment in Paris I always dreamed about, with a piano and a terrace.'

But how would she do that? She had no money, no resources, and if she was free from him, her father might plan another marriage for her. But maybe Halina would prefer that, rather than be shackled to him for the rest of her life. The knowledge hurt, far more than Rico wanted it to.

'Well, then,' he said in a hard voice. 'Now we're prepared for the worst. So let's hope for the best, hey? And keep you on bed rest.'

She smiled faintly. 'In control, as always.'

'Yes,' Rico answered, but he didn't feel in control at all. Now, more than ever, he felt as if things were spinning out of his grasp…especially his own heart.

CHAPTER FOURTEEN

TODAY WOULD HAVE been her wedding day. Halina gazed out of the window of her bedroom at the buildings and streets of the Eternal City, feeling more in limbo now than ever. The last week had been endless, lying in bed, waiting for the worst to happen.

Since the first terror-filled visit to the hospital, thankfully she hadn't had any more episodes of bleeding, but she still lived in fear, and so did Rico. They were both tiptoeing around each other, a constant strain between them, caused, Halina supposed, by the new uncertainty that had opened up like a yawning chasm, sending them both into tense isolation.

Any day, any week, and it could all be over. Their child's life, the little family they'd been creating, the marriage they'd both intended to embark on. All of it could be reduced to nothing. It was exhausting, living with that kind of uncertainty, and Halina spent most of her enforced bed rest sleeping, in part just to escape the strain. How long would it last? The next five months? Or maybe not long at all. Maybe today would be the day it ended. It was impossible to know.

What she did know was that she'd fallen in love with Rico and it was tearing her apart. At every turn her fears were confirmed and the knowledge that he didn't love her, didn't want to love her, reverberated through her all over again, a loss she could never get used to. A tiny, treacherous part of her almost wondered if losing this baby would bring its own bitter relief, because then she wouldn't be faced with a loveless future with Rico. She hated herself for thinking that way for even a single second, and guilt scorched through her, making her even more miserable.

Rico had berated her for not taking care of herself, and had tried to make her eat when she had no appetite due to fear and worry. She knew he was feeling it too, and she wished they could comfort each other in their shared anxiety and sorrow. But that never seemed to be the case; like the ninth circle of Dante's terrible hell, they were frozen in their own isolation, doomed to a life of loneliness.

The sound of the intercom of the flat buzzing had Halina turning from the window in surprise. Rico was at work, and no one called at the flat; deliveries were left with the building's doorman.

Cautiously she went to answer the intercom. 'Hello?'

'*Signorina?*' The doorman's disembodied voice came through the speaker. 'You have a visitor.'

'A visitor…?'

'Sultan Hassan Amar,' the doorman said in a tone of utmost respect. 'He says he is your father.'

For a few seconds Halina couldn't think. She

couldn't even breathe. She simply stood there, blinking, one finger pressed down on the intercom.

'*Signorina?*'

'Yes, I'm here.' Her voice sounded strangely tinny and faraway. 'Send him up.'

As soon as she'd said the words she half-regretted them. What if her father was here to take her back home against Rico's wishes? What if she got kidnapped yet again? But then she reasoned that he wouldn't have come to do such a thing on his own. And in any case, if he was on his own she could resist. If she wanted to.

The treacherous flicker of wanting made her pause. Could she really be thinking that way, even for a moment?

The lift doors pinged open and then her father stepped into the open area of the penthouse. Halina turned to him, her mind spinning, her heart beating wildly as her throat dried.

'Father.'

'Halina.' His gaze dipped down to the gentle swell of her belly. 'You are looking well.'

'Am I?' She laughed uncertainly because lately, despite all the rest, she'd been looking as worn out as an old dishrag. 'I don't feel all that well.'

'You don't? Is something wrong?'

The note of alarm in her father's voice caught her on the raw. 'Why do you care?' she couldn't keep herself from retorting bitterly. 'You never wanted this baby to live.'

Her father's face contorted with a spasm of grief and he started towards her, his arms outstretched. 'Halina, *habibi*...'

'Don't.' Halina stepped back quickly, nearly tripping over her own feet. 'Why are you here, Father?'

'I was intending to come to your wedding, and then Falcone informed me he'd called it off.'

She flinched, in part because of the stark fact of her father's words, and in part because Rico hadn't even told her that her father had called, or that he'd changed his mind and had been planning on coming to their wedding after all. The relationship between her and Rico, if she could even call it that, had broken down even more than she'd realised... But perhaps nothing had been built up enough to be broken. It had all been in her head, the intimacy, emotion and love. All on her side.

'Why don't you sit down, Halina?' her father suggested gently. 'And let us talk.'

She wrapped her arms around herself, feeling cold despite the warm October day. 'What do we have to talk about?'

'There is much I wish to say to you. Much I sincerely regret.'

Halina hesitated, then she nodded. 'All right.' They moved towards a pair of luxurious grey suede sofas; she'd spent many happy evenings there curled up next to Rico, watching television or reading a book, pleasant hours they'd whiled away together. It felt like a dream world now.

'What is it?'

'I want to apologise for my conduct to you,' Hassan said seriously. 'I regret the way I acted very much.' He bowed his head, seemingly overcome, and Halina stared at him, too shocked to feel gratified or hopeful. Yet.

'Do you...do you really mean that?'

Hassan looked up, tears gleaming in his dark eyes. 'Yes, I do. Events overtook me, my daughter, and I let them carry me away. I couldn't think properly with everything that had happened. Prince Zayed's kidnapping attempt, your situation... There was so much to deal with.'

'I know,' Halina whispered. 'For me too, Father. And I... I know I acted improperly. Recklessly. I regret that very much. I do.'

'And I acted recklessly as well,' the Sultan returned seriously. 'But let us have no more regrets, Halina. Now that the wedding is called off, I am here to take you home.'

Halina stared at her father in shock, his words penetrating her overwhelmed state and leaving her cold. 'Take me home...?'

'Where you belong. Where you'll be happy. This is no place for you.'

'Rico Falcone is the father of my child.'

'I have had investigators research his past,' Hassan returned, his tone becoming cold. 'Do you know this man, Halina? Do you really know him?'

She loved him. 'What did you find out?'

'That he grew up a gutter rat, and then made his fortune in property investments, and has been known for years as being a cold, ruthless, heartless man. That he has had many women, more than you can imagine, and they never lasted for more than a week. That he has been quoted as saying he doesn't believe in love and he doesn't have time for marriage. This is not a man you want to marry, *habibi*.'

Nothing her father had said about Rico was a surprise to her, but to hear it spelt out so plainly, so terribly... It was hard to bear. Hard to accept. And yet Halina knew she had to.

'This is not the man for you,' Hassan said definitively. 'Or for your child.'

'Rico would never leave his child,' Halina said, unsure what she was really saying. That he would leave her? That she wanted to go but couldn't? She felt a welter of confusion and grief, and it didn't help that things had been so strained between Rico and her recently. She was filled with doubt and fear.

'Are you sure about that?' Hassan asked, his tone gentle. 'Has he said so?'

'He took me from the Palace of Forgotten Sands,' Halina reminded him bitterly. 'Where you'd left me to rot.'

'That is not true, *habibi*. I put you there to keep you safe.'

Her father had a penchant for viewing things through his own singular lens. He always had. It hadn't mattered when she'd been treated like a spoilt pet, but now it made a difference.

'That's what it felt like, Father,' Halina said quietly. 'And I don't have any desire to return to such circumstances.'

'That's not what I'm suggesting at all,' Hassan protested. 'Halina, I am asking you to return to your home, your family. Your sisters long to see you, and so does your mother.'

'You forbade me from seeing my sisters.'

Hassan bowed his head. 'An impetuous decision that I regret. Halina, come home. We all want you to come home. Falcone can't force you to stay here, and in all truth I suspect he would be relieved if you left. Such a man is not made for marriage and family.'

Halina flinched, because her father was only voicing her own terrible suspicions. What if they were both right? What if Rico secretly wanted her to go? Yes, he had a protective streak a mile wide, and he'd been determined to look after her and their baby. But she didn't sense any joy from him, any gladness that he had to do it, that she was here. In her darkest moments she'd even wondered if Rico would be relieved if things ended, if they had no child together.

'Halina,' Hassan said gently. 'I have the royal jet at the airport. We can be heading back to Abkar, to your family, in an hour.'

She ached to see her sisters, her mother. To feel safe and loved, instead of restless and uncertain.

'I can't leave without telling Rico,' she said, hardly able to believe she was saying the words.

'Telling me what?' Rico demanded as he stepped through the doors of the lift and surveyed them both with a dark glare.

Rico gazed between Sultan Hassan's impassive face and Halina's frightened and confused one and felt his stomach and jaw both clench. Whatever they'd been talking about, it hadn't been good.

'What do you need to tell me, Halina?' he asked in as mild a voice as he could manage. 'What's going on?'

'Tell him, *habibi*,' the Sultan said.

The endearment did not go unnoticed. So that was how Hassan was playing it. The doting father had returned. Rico had often wondered how he would act if his father had ever returned. What he would have said, whether he would have opened his arms to him. He'd known what Halina would do. He saw it in her face, in the unhappy guilt written on her delicate features.

She was leaving him. At least, she was thinking about it. God knew the last few weeks had been hard. He knew that; he'd felt it. Halina's admission that she wanted love from him, from their marriage, the terrible uncertainty shrouding her pregnancy...all of it had taken its toll. Had made her doubt, made them both doubt, if they were doing the right thing getting married. Because he was honest enough to admit he'd started wondering too, and somehow that made this moment all the harder to bear.

'Halina?' he prompted, an edge entering his voice, and she stared at him unhappily, her lips trembling.

'Let me talk to him,' the Sultan said, and Rico swung his gaze over to appraise his real adversary. He didn't trust this man. Not a single inch.

'I can…' Halina persisted, but she looked so pale and miserable that Rico took pity on her.

'Let him say what he wants to say. We can talk later if needed. You should rest.'

They stared at each other for a long moment, a world of yearning and regret spinning out between them, then she nodded and walked wordlessly to the bedroom. As the door clicked shut behind her Rico turned to face Hassan.

'Well?' he said coolly.

'The Princess is coming home with me.'

Rico kept his expression neutral, refusing to give the man the satisfaction of seeing him affected by anything he said. 'That was your suggestion, I presume?' he drawled.

'My suggestion and her desire.'

'She said as much?'

'I know it. She's my daughter.'

'And she's the mother of my child.' Rico stared at the man, refusing so much as to blink. 'We are to be married.'

'Yet the wedding was called off.'

'For health reasons only.'

'Come now, Falcone.' Hassan smiled, the genial expression so close to a smirk that Rico itched to wipe it off his face. His fists clenched and he forced himself to unclench them and relax. 'Let's be honest with each other, now it is just the two of us.'

'I am being honest.'

The smile dropped from Hassan's face like the mask Rico had known it was. 'I have had people look into you and your background,' he said in a low voice, his lip curling in an ugly sneer. 'Seen what a gutter rat you truly are. No matter how many billions you have now, you were born a beggar boy and you still are one now. I will never allow you to marry my daughter, a princess of the royal blood. How could I?'

'What you will allow is not my concern. Halina is of age and in this country, my country, she is not bound by your archaic laws.' Rico spoke calmly even though the blood was boiling through his veins.

'So you would shackle her to you, all because of a child you've never wanted?'

'I'll always want my child.'

'Oh, yes, I understand that certain code of honour—'

'Do you?' Rico interjected, unable to keep the venom from his voice. 'Because, by all accounts, you do not possess it.'

'Halina has spoken to you about that unfortunate incident, I see.'

'You tried to make your own daughter get an abortion she didn't want.'

'I am King of a country, Falcone,' Hassan said

sharply. 'With it comes responsibilities and expectations, some of them unfortunate. For my people to see my own daughter shamed in such a way…it would be disastrous. For them, for my rule, for the stability of my country and for Halina herself.' He took a step towards Rico. 'She sees things from her own view, a simple child's view. Trust me, the truth is much more complicated. But we are both men of the world. We know that.'

Rico stared at him, his jaw clenched so tight he thought he might break a tooth. He recognised the truth in the Sultan's words, a truth he had not wanted to see before. He didn't condone the man's actions; he could never do that. But he could understand them.

'Halina belongs in Abkar with her own people, her own family.'

'And would you marry her off to a man of your choosing, a stranger?' Rico demanded. 'Because those do not seem the actions of the loving father you are professing to be now.'

'Come, Falcone.' Hassan smiled. 'We both know that her marriage to you would be no different, and in some ways worse, for there would be no political benefit to you. You would tire of her eventually, whether you are willing to acknowledge it or not.' The Sultan levelled him with a starkly honest and challenging stare. 'Do you honestly think you could ever make her happy?'

Rico tried not to flinch at that question and the lack it revealed in himself. Because the truth that he'd been trying to avoid staring in the face for the last few weeks was that he didn't. And he knew in his gut, in his heart, that Halina deserved more than he could ever give her.

'Would you marry her off against her will?' he asked, the words dragged from him, scraping his throat.

'Against her will? No. In time, when she has recovered from this and longs for a husband and a family? We would make the decision together. That much I have learned.' The Sultan met his gaze unblinkingly; Rico knew he had no choice but to trust him.

'And the child?' he asked painfully, the sting of tears behind his lids, in the back of his throat.

'Would want for nothing. He or she would grow up in the palace, a member of the royal family.'

'Your people would accept that?'

Hassan smiled grimly. 'They will have to.'

Several moments ticked by; it took all of Rico's energy and effort simply to breathe. To keep standing. 'Fine,' he said finally. 'Leave us now. I want to talk to Halina.'

'I'll return in an hour.'

'An hour…'

'It will be better if it's quick,' the Sultan said, then walked towards the lift.

Rico stood where he was, waiting for the man to leave before he moved. Before he told Halina what he intended.

As the doors pinged open and then shut Rico let

out a shuddering breath. So this would be the end. He would let her go, because he cared for her too much to shackle her to him. He saw that now.

And, in a jolt of sorrowful realisation, it occurred to him that he finally had a glimmer of understanding of what his father might have gone through in leaving him at the orphanage all those years ago.

Perhaps, just as Rico had, his father had come to the grief-filled conclusion that he could not make the person he loved most in the world happy. That he could not provide for them in the way he longed to. That leaving was the better, and harder, choice.

With a leaden heart, Rico walked towards the bedroom door.

CHAPTER FIFTEEN

HALINA HEARD THE rise and fall of low, tense voices from behind the door but she couldn't make out any words and she didn't think she wanted to. What was her father saying to Rico? And what was Rico saying to her father?

She paced the room in a ferment of anxiety and fear, wondering if the two men she loved most in the world were deciding her future without her. Here, then, was the ultimate loss of freedom. Her fate was completely out of her hands, even while she waited in the next room.

Then she heard the lift doors open and closing. She stilled where she was by the window, one hand resting on the sill. She couldn't hear a sound from the other room; had Rico gone?

Just when she was about to go and find him, the bedroom door opened and Rico stood there. The haggard and grim look on his face struck a cold note of fear in Halina's heart.

'Rico…'

'Your father will return in an hour.'

'Return? Why?'

'It's better this way, Halina.'

'Better?' She stared at him wildly. The doubts that had been festering in her heart burst into painful reality. 'What are you saying? You want me to go?'

'It's not a question of want or whim. It's what is best for you—'

'Best for you, you mean!' Halina cried, pain lancing every word.

'I can't give you what you need.'

'You mean you can't love me.' Even now it hurt to say it. Rico hesitated, his jaw tight, and then he nodded. 'And what if I was willing to live with that?' Halina asked painfully.

'Do you remember what you said to me? That if my loyalty or affection wasn't grounded in love it would eventually fade?'

'Yes, but—'

'Are you no different? Eventually you would come to resent me for not loving you. Hate me, even. And I would hate that. So would you. We'd end up living separate lives, festering in bitterness and resentment.'

She stared at him, hating the bleak, bleak picture he painted with his grim words. 'It wouldn't have to be like that.'

'Maybe not, but the risk is too great. I can't make you happy, Halina. I can't give you what you want.'

'And that is a reason to walk away?' she demanded, her voice shaking. 'You're a coward, Rico Falcone—'

'Do you think this is easy for me?' he cut across her, his voice a ragged roar. 'Do you think I am doing this lightly? I am talking of abandoning my child, as my father once abandoned me. Do you think I would ever want to do that?'

'Then don't—'

'I am trying to do the right thing, hard as it is for both of us. You have to think of the future, Halina. Your future. Perhaps one day you'll find a man you love, a man who can make you happy…'

'Perhaps,' Halina answered in a choked voice, 'happiness is overrated.'

Rico stared at her. 'Do you really mean that?'

Halina simply stared back, confused and miserable. She didn't know anything any more. She didn't understand why Rico was doing this, even as she feared she did. Because their relationship had been doomed from the start—forced into a marriage neither of them wanted for a child they never should have conceived. But even now she couldn't regret her baby, their baby, and she pressed a trembling hand against the soft swell of her bump.

'What of your child? What shall I tell him or her about you?' She shook her head slowly. 'You're really going to give up all your rights?'

'It's better this way,' Rico said. His face was as blank as his voice; it was as if he had already left her, emotionally if not physically. Halina knew she would never reach him.

'So that's it?' she said hollowly. 'After everything

that's happened…the way you pursued me, how determined you were to marry me…that's it?'

A full minute ticked by as Rico stared at her, his jaw clenched, his eyes pitilessly blank. 'That's it,' he said flatly.

Everything happened in a fast, unhappy blur after that. Halina packed, leaving behind the couture gowns and outfits that she and Rico had shopped for together. She couldn't bear to bring away clothes that held so many memories, beautiful as they were. Her father arrived, nodding graciously to Rico before he turned to Halina.

'Are you ready, *habibi*? The plane is waiting. So is your family. I called your mother and she is eager to see you.'

Everything in Halina cried out to resist. She stood in the living room, trying to work up the courage to turn to Rico and tell him she loved him. She'd never said the words. She'd never confessed how she felt about him, only that she wanted him to love her. Would it make a difference? Didn't she have a duty to try?

She opened her mouth, her heart beating hard, but before she could say a word Rico spoke first.

'Goodbye,' he said, and walked out of the room.

Halina stood there for a moment, stunned and blinking, then she followed her father out of the apartment.

She didn't talk much on the ride to the airport; grief swamped her, a fog surrounding her that made it difficult to think, much less speak.

Sultan Hassan was all gracious solicitude, asking
how she felt, if there was anything she needed. Once
they were on the royal jet Halina went to lie down;
she couldn't face anyone, not even the servants. She
slept the entire journey, only waking up when it was
time to land.

She stared out of the window of the jet at the bleak,
undulating desert of Abkar and her heart cried out
for Rome. For Rico.

'Everyone is waiting for you,' Hassan said as he
guided her from the jet to the waiting SUV. Halina
slid inside, resting her head against the seat. She felt
too listless to ask what was going to happen now,
what her father intended.

Would she live in the royal palace? Raise her child
there, under the benevolent eyes of her parents? It was
so far from the fury and sick disappointment they'd
shown her before, she couldn't quite believe in it.
Somehow it didn't much matter any more, because
Rico had rejected her.

Throughout the journey, even as she remained
dazed, one hard truth had emerged from the fog of
her mind. His claim that he was thinking of her, of
her happiness, was nothing more than an excuse. Of
course it was. Rico would never give up his child unless he wanted to. Unless he'd decided that marriage
and fatherhood wasn't for him, after all.

Bitterness rooted in her heart as she replayed their
last conversation in her mind. He was a coward. He
should have had the courage to tell her the truth—that

he'd changed his mind, that he didn't want to marry her—instead of dressing it up with fine sentiments about thinking only of her happiness.

Back at the palace her sisters swarmed her, and Halina hugged each of them in turn, her heart emerging from its chrysalis of grief as she realised afresh how much she'd missed her family.

'Halina.' Aliya pressed her cheek against her daughter's. 'We are so glad you have returned home.'

'Thank you, Mother,' Halina whispered.

'We have much to do,' Aliya said as she gestured for Halina to sit down in the family's private living area. A member of staff poured glasses of mint tea.

'Much to do?' Halina's youngest sister was curled up on her lap and Halina put her arms around her, grateful for the easy affection.

'Yes, for the wedding.' Halina stared blankly at her mother and Aliya's eyes narrowed. 'To the Sultan of Bahari. Surely your father told you?'

'No,' Halina said numbly. 'He didn't tell me.'

'But the wedding is in a week! The Sultan wants to marry you before you show too much.' With her lips pressed together, Aliya glanced repressively at her younger daughters. 'You are lucky to have such a match arranged for you, Halina.'

'Lucky?' Halina stared at her mother in disbelief as realisation bloomed poisonously inside her. Her father had duped her with his words of love and regret. He'd wanted her home only so he could marry her off again to his political advantage, this time to a man over three times her age.

She knew the Sultan of Bahari. She'd sat next to him at one of those stuffy diplomatic receptions; he had to be at least seventy, and he had two wives already. And it seemed she was to be the third. Bile churned in her stomach and rose in her throat.

'Mother,' she whispered, 'Are you really intending this for me?'

Aliya folded her arms. 'It is all you have left.'

'Rico Falcone, the father of my child, a billionaire in his own right, was willing to marry me,' Halina retorted, even as a treacherous little voice inside whispered, *Was he?* 'Surely he is more appropriate than an aging lecher with two wives already?'

'Do not speak so disrespectfully. Falcone is not appropriate because he does not offer any political alliances, and his reputation is quite beyond the pale. This is your duty, Halina. Surely you see that? After all your disgrace, this is the least you can do for your family.'

The *least*? She'd be giving up her whole life, and in far worse a way than any future she could have envisioned with Rico. But Rico didn't want her, and Halina was left yet again with no freedom, no choice, in the worst situation she'd ever had to face.

She turned from her mother, tears blurring her eyes. She could hardly believe she was right back where she started, only worse. So much worse.

Rico. Her heart cried out his name. She should

have told him she loved him. Even if she had to marry the Sultan of Bahari, at least Rico would have known. It would have been small comfort during the bleak, barren years that stretched ahead of her now.

Three days had passed since Halina had walked out of his flat, his life. Three endless days. It was long enough for Rico to reconsider his decision, which now seemed unaccountably rash. What had he been thinking of, letting her go? Letting his child go?

Sultan Hassan had played on all his doubts, all his fears of inadequacy and commitment. The fear he had of risking his heart for someone, holding it there for her to crack or crush. Halina had been right. He was a coward. He'd chosen to let her go rather than fight to hold on. To tell her the truth, which had come to him in a shocking moment of naked realisation: that he loved her. He'd loved her for a while, but he'd been hiding it from himself because he'd been so afraid. Afraid to fall, to risk, to beg her to stay. So he'd chosen the cowardly option of walking away.

Now he would live the rest of his life knowing he'd loved and lost. It was the price of his cowardice, his shame. And all he could do was pray and hope that she had a better life without him.

Then, on the fourth day after Halina's departure, Rico read the headline in the society section of the newspaper: *Abkaran Princess to Marry Sultan.*

Everything in him stilled as he scanned the few scant lines.

Princess Halina of Abkar, recently engaged to billionaire tycoon Rico Falcone, is now poised to marry the Sultan of Bahari on Saturday. The Sultan has two wives already, and the Princess will be his third.

Rico's head jerked up from the newspaper, shock slamming into him, leaving him breathless. The *third* wife? He glanced back down at the article and saw a grainy black-and-white photograph of the Sultan, a paunchy old man with jowly cheeks and a smug smile. His skin crawled. He hadn't let go of Halina for this. He hadn't sacrificed his own happiness, his own heart, for her to be married off to some old lecher.

And he was sure, with a stony certainty, that she hadn't known what she was walking into when she'd returned to Abkar. Her father had tricked them both.

Rico swore out loud, viciously and fluently. His emotional cowardice had led to this disaster. He'd wanted the very best for Halina, and instead he'd dumped her in the worst situation possible. With his mouth hardening into a grim line of determination, Rico reached for his phone. He'd rescued Halina once before. He could do it again. Only this time it might take a little more finesse.

Several hours later, Rico had found his way forward thanks to a few crucial phone calls. He booked a flight to Bahari and within hours of landing he had a royal audience with the Sultan. Forty-five minutes later, their business was concluded and, after spending the night at a hotel in the desert country's capital city, he booked another flight to Abkar.

He stood in front of the royal palace, soldiers barring his way, the golden stone of the palace shimmering under the hot desert sun.

'You may tell the Sultan I am here in regard to Princess Halina's forthcoming marriage. I have crucial news that I know he will want to hear.'

The soldiers glared at him uncertainly before one gave a terse nod and spoke Arabic into an intercom. Several tense minutes later Rico was admitted to the palace and led to a small, spartan waiting room.

The Sultan kept him waiting for nearly an hour before he finally deigned to make an appearance. Rico didn't mind. He wasn't going to play the man's petty games, and he wasn't going to fall prey to them either. Not any more.

'How surprising to see you here,' the Sultan remarked, his eyes cold, any pretence at friendliness dropped. 'I cannot begin to imagine what you have to say to me in regard to the Princess's marriage, but I decided to humour you.' He folded his arms. 'So, say what you will and then be gone.'

'The Sultan of Bahari has called off the marriage.'

Hassan's eyes narrowed. 'You are talking nonsense.'

'I am not. If you wish for it to be confirmed, you may call him.' He held out his phone, his eyes glinting with challenge. 'I have access to his private line.'

'What have you done?' Hassan ground out, staring at Rico's phone as if it were a snake poised to strike.

'Why don't you find out?'

Wordlessly Hassan snatched the phone and swiped to dial. Seconds later they both heard ringing and then the Sultan of Bahari's unctuous voice. Hassan listened for several taut seconds, his expression becoming grimmer and grimmer, before he ended the call and flung the phone at Rico. Rico caught it neatly.

'Very clever, Falcone. Very clever.'

'It is too bad for you that the Sultan prefers race-horses to wives.'

'How much did it cost you to buy him that horse?' Hassan asked scornfully. 'Millions? Money wasted. I am not letting Halina go.'

'Yes, you are,' Rico said evenly. 'Because, if you don't, I will do everything in my power, give everything I have, to ruin you. And trust me, Hassan, it can be done. I've only just begun, and I enjoy a challenge.'

Hassan stared at him for a long moment, his eyes cold, his jaw tight. 'What does it matter so much to you?' he finally asked. 'You've had dozens—no, hundreds—of women. She's but one. Why can't you leave her alone?'

'If she wants me to leave her alone, I will. But that's her choice,' Rico returned. 'Not yours.'

Another minute passed, taut with suppressed tension and resentment. Then Hassan shrugged. 'Fine. She's damaged goods anyway, and I would be hard pressed to find someone suitable to take her now. Do what you like with her, but she will not be welcome back here.'

'That,' Rico answered, 'is your loss.'

A short while later he stood in front of the doors to a more ornate reception room, his heart beginning to hammer as doubt chased him yet again. He'd acted precipitously, out of concern for Halina, but what if it had cost her her family? What if she would have rather married the damned Sultan? There was only one way to find out.

Taking a deep breath, Rico opened the doors. Halina was standing on the far side of the room, once again looking pale and gaunt despite the roundness of her belly. She whirled around as he came into the room, her mouth dropping open in shock.

'Rico...'

'Did your father not tell you I was here?'

'No one's told me anything.' She drew a shuddering breath. 'I'm to marry the Sultan of Bahari...'

'No, you're not. The wedding's off.'

She stared at him in confusion. 'What?'

'I made a deal with the Sultan of Bahari. He agreed to call off the wedding, in exchange for a racehorse he has been wanting for many years.'

'A racehorse!'

'The owner wouldn't sell it to him, so I bought it instead.'

'How...?'

'It is done easily enough, when you know the right

people and offer the right amount of money. But first, Halina, tell me you're all right. The baby…'

'The baby's all right.' She gave him a wan, tremulous smile. 'I haven't had any more bleeding and I've felt movement—tiny little flutters.'

'Thank God.'

'But why are you here, Rico? Why have you done this?'

'Because I read about your engagement in the newspaper and I didn't believe for a second that you wanted that. I feared your father had tricked you into coming home.'

'He did.' Halina closed her eyes briefly. 'I should have known better.'

'*Cara,* so should I. I will never forgive myself for jeopardising your life, your happiness, in such a way.'

'Let's have no more recriminations, please, Rico. There has been far too much regret already.'

'I need to ask.' Rico looked at her seriously. 'Is this what you want? Because your father made it clear that, if you left with me, you would not be welcomed back by your family. It's a high price to pay, Halina, and one I should have foreseen. Only you can decide if you wish to pay it.'

'And what is the alternative?' she asked, staring at him with wide, troubled eyes. 'To marry a man old enough to be my grandfather, and live in shame and seclusion as his third wife with an illegitimate child that would no doubt be taken away from me? Rico, it's a hard price to pay, but I pay it willingly. You need not fear that.'

'Good.' He took her hands, which felt small and icy, in his. 'Then it's time we departed.'

'Are we going back to Rome?'

'No,' Rico said, his heart full of both love and pain. He finally knew what love was, and he understood it was so much more than he'd thought. It wasn't an ephemeral emotion; it was life itself, duty and sacrifice, joy and feeling. He would do anything for Halina because he loved her. He would even let her go.

'Rico…? Where are we going?'

He smiled at her, his heart aching with both love and loss. 'We're going to Paris.'

CHAPTER SIXTEEN

YET AGAIN, WITHIN the space of a week, Halina found herself on a private jet, crossing the world. She felt such an overwhelming mix of relief and sadness that she could barely begin to process the emotions. To have seen her sisters, her family, again only to say goodbye so soon. It filled her with grief, even as she acknowledged the sweet and overwhelming relief at being rescued from a fate so grim she hated even to imagine it.

But what was going to happen now? She'd asked Rico why they were going to Paris, but he'd refused to be drawn. And, instead of seeming happy to have got her back, he'd withdrawn even more into himself, seeming so quiet and sad that Halina feared the cost her rescue was to him. Were they really better off than they'd been a few days ago before her father had arrived? It felt as if nothing had really changed; Rico was still remote and she still loved him. An impossible situation.

The plane finally touched down in Paris and, as they drove into the city, Halina gazed out of the limo's window in awe and wonder, her nose nearly pressed to the glass.

'There's the Eiffel Tower!' she exclaimed. 'I've only seen it in pictures…'

'You'll have time to do all the sightseeing you want,' Rico assured her, and she turned back to him uncertainly. Why did he sound so resigned?

Realisation began to dawn when the limo turned onto a street of eighteenth-century townhouses, tall and elegant. It parked in front of number eighteen, a lovely old building covered in vines, just like in the children's story *Madeline*.

'What…?' Halina began in a disbelieving whisper. Rico drew a key from his pocket.

'Come,' he said, and she followed him out of the limo and up the stairs to the front door painted a shiny red. 'Sorry, there are quite a few stairs,' he remarked as he fitted the key in the door. 'But you did say the top floor.'

'My dream…' she whispered, feeling as if she were in one. She followed Rico into an old-fashioned lift with a grille for a door, up to the flat on the top floor. He unlocked the door and ushered her inside.

Halina stepped into the little hallway with its antique flocked wallpaper and colourful prints. She turned the corner and gazed in amazement at the living room—the squashy sofa, the grand piano, the shelves of books. It was as if he'd conjured it straight out of her head.

'How did you…?' she began, walking slowly

around the apartment. There was a cosy kitchen with dishes in different colours and fresh flowers on the table. The bedroom had a double bed with a cover decorated in *broderie anglaise*, the window's bright-blue shutters open to the October sunshine.

And the balcony… She pushed open the French windows from the living room and stepped onto the tiny balcony with its wrought-iron railings and pots of herbs and flowers. Below her the streets of the Latin Quarter bustled and the smell of freshly baked croissants drifted up. Halina turned to Rico, shaking her head in amazement.

'It's as if you pulled this right out of my dreams.'

'Well, you did describe it to me in some detail.' He smiled faintly, but his eyes still looked sad.

'Yes, but how did you arrange it all?'

'It took some doing. I had very specific requests.' Rico's smile deepened. 'But it was worth it.'

'Rico, I don't know what to say.'

'The deed is in your name, of course,' he continued, and Halina blinked.

'What?'

'I've engaged a housekeeper to come once a week, but of course that's up to you. I thought you'd want your privacy.'

'I don't understand.'

'Of course this place might feel small once the baby comes, but we can cross that bridge when you come to it. If you'd like to move somewhere more suitable eventually, it can be arranged.'

'Now I really don't understand.' Her voice and body both shook. 'What are you telling me, Rico?'

He smiled sadly. 'I'm giving you what you've always wanted, Halina. Your freedom.'

Rico watched Halina's eyes widen in shock. Seeing her delight in the little flat had brought him such painful joy. She would be happy here. He'd make sure of it. Because, when you loved someone, you wanted their happiness more than anything. More than your own.

'My freedom,' Halina repeated slowly. 'You mean, you're leaving me again?'

'I'm giving you what you want,' Rico insisted. He'd thought long and hard about what to do when he'd been flying to Bahari and then Abkar. What Halina needed to be happy. 'You told me—many times you told me—that you wanted your freedom, the chance to choose your own destiny. Well, here it is.'

'But I'm not choosing it,' Halina said, her voice growing in force and volume. 'Am I? You're still choosing it for me.'

Rico blinked, surprised by her fury. He'd thought she'd be pleased. He'd wanted to please her. Or, he wondered with an uncomfortable pang, had he been trying to assuage his own guilty conscience for backing out on her once before?

'If you don't want to live here, you don't have to.'

'I thought… I thought when you came for me you'd come to bring me back with you, because that's where you wanted me.' Her breath thickened. 'With you.'

'I'm trying to do the right thing, Halina—'

'Are you? Or are you trying to do the safe thing? Rico, I love you.'

The words fell into the shocked stillness.

'I've loved you for a while, and I should have told you sooner, but I was afraid. But I don't want to be afraid any longer. I've been batted back and forth like a ball in a game and I don't want that either. I want the freedom to choose, yes, and I choose you. If you'll have me.'

His stunned mind couldn't make sense of her words.

She continued determinedly. 'I know you don't love me, and I'm willing to accept that. I hope in time you might at least come to care for me a little, but in the meantime I want what we had before. I'll let it be enough. I want us, Rico. I want our family.'

'Stop.' His voice was so choked he could barely get the single word out. 'Stop, Halina. I can't let you say any more.'

Her eyes clouded and her lips trembled. 'You can't?'

'No, because you're wrong. So wrong. I won't come to care for you a little in time, because I'm already completely, hopelessly in love with you.' Her mouth dropped open and he started walking towards her. 'I've been fighting it for a while, maybe even since we first met. Fighting it, because I was so scared of loving someone again, letting myself get hurt. Left. And so I did what I thought I'd never, ever do and I left you instead. I convinced myself I was doing the right thing, the noble thing, but really it was just cowardice. You were right to call me a coward, Halina. *Lina.* My Lina.'

He took hold of her hands, drawing her towards him. 'To hear that you love me…to know it and believe it… I wish I'd told you first. I wish I'd had that much courage. But I'm so honoured, so privileged, to be loved by you. I don't deserve it. I know I don't.'

'Deserving doesn't come into it, Rico,' Halina said softly as she came into his arms. 'Love is a gift, freely given, gratefully received. And that's how it is for me.'

'And for me. I love you so much. So much.'

'And I love you just as much.'

He kissed her then, because he needed to feel her in his arms, against his mouth. Halina wound her arms around his neck, her pliant body pressed to his as the sun spilled through the windows, and the whole world sang.

EPILOGUE

Six months later

'HE'S A HUNGRY little fellow, isn't he?' Rico gazed down at his son's rosebud mouth sucking greedily at his mother's breast. Halina stroked her baby's hair and looked up with laughing eyes.

'I don't mind.'

'As long as you're getting enough rest.'

'Plenty.' They shared a loving smile as he touched her hand, still incredulous, and so incredibly grateful, that she was here. That they shared this rare and precious happiness.

The last six months had been tumultuous, with their quiet wedding ceremony taking place when Halina had been seven months pregnant. Her friend Olivia, wife to Prince Zayed, had come, as had her husband, and Rico had found he liked the man. Halina's mother had come too, the first step of many to healing her fractured family.

After ten gruelling hours of labour his son, Matteo Falcone, had been born. Named after Rico's father, because all this had taught him that everyone made mistakes as well as hard choices. He didn't know which his father had made, but he knew he finally had it in his heart to forgive him. Because of Halina, and the light and love she'd brought to his life. The healing.

'I think he's had enough.' Halina lifted their sleepy son up to him. 'Do you want to hold him?'

'Of course.' Rico never tired of cradling his precious, tiny son. He marvelled that marriage and family had been gifts, treasures that he'd scorned, and he thanked God that he'd learned otherwise.

Now he balanced Matteo on his shoulder and gently jiggled him while Halina watched, a faint smile curving her face. She'd blossomed in the last few months through a difficult pregnancy, a tough labour, and then moving house to the villa outside Rome where they lived now, perfect for a growing family. Through it all she'd grown in grace and beauty, basking in his love for her, a love he'd never tire of showing and feeling…even when life was hard. Especially when it was.

'What are you thinking?' Halina asked softly, and Rico smiled.

'How blessed I am.'

'And I am, as well.'

'Yes, we both are.' He drew her up from the rocking chair and put his arm around her so they were together in a tight circle, the people he loved most in the world. His family. Their family. Together at last for ever.

* * * * *

COMING NEXT MONTH FROM
HARLEQUIN
Presents®

Available September 18, 2018

#3657 BILLIONAIRE'S BABY OF REDEMPTION
Rings of Vengeance
by Michelle Smart

When Javier learns his explosive night with Sophie left her pregnant, he's adamant they wed! But warm, compassionate Sophie demands more. Can Javier accept that giving her and the baby his all is the key to his redemption?

#3658 THE ITALIAN'S UNEXPECTED LOVE-CHILD
Secret Heirs of Billionaires
by Miranda Lee

A luxury villa will be the latest jewel in Leonardo's crown, until he discovers Veronica stands to inherit it. Their chemistry is spectacular...but so are the consequences when Veronica reveals she's pregnant!

#3659 CONSEQUENCE OF THE GREEK'S REVENGE
One Night With Consequences
by Trish Morey

Wary of being exploited for her fortune, Athena is devastated to learn Alexios only wants her to avenge himself against her father! But when the consequence of their passion is revealed, he wants her for so much more...

#3660 BOUND BY A ONE-NIGHT VOW
Conveniently Wed!
by Melanie Milburne

Isabella is on a deadline. She has twenty-four hours to wed or she'll lose her inheritance! Andrea knows she can't refuse his proposition for a temporary union. But can Izzy risk surrendering to temptation?

#3661 SHEIKH'S PRINCESS OF CONVENIENCE
Bound to the Desert King
by Dani Collins

Entertaining Princess Galila at a royal wedding seems frivolous... until she reveals Karim's family's darkest secret. To prevent a scandal, Karim will make Galila his convenient bride!

#3662 THE SPANIARD'S PLEASURABLE VENGEANCE
by Lucy Monroe

Poised to bring the Perez name into disrepute, Miranda must be stopped! But when Basilio meets Miranda, he is captivated. His plan becomes one of seduction...that tests his control to the limit!

#3663 KIDNAPPED FOR HER SECRET SON
by Andie Brock

When Jaco discovers Leah's given birth to his heir, he's determined to shield them from his adoptive family's criminal intentions! He kidnaps Leah and his son, whisking them away to his island...

#3664 THE TYCOON'S ULTIMATE CONQUEST
by Cathy Williams

Arturo is furious when Rose places his latest business deal in jeopardy. Now his greatest asset will be seduction, leaving Rose so overwhelmed with pleasure that she forgets all about the deal. Until he finds himself equally addicted—to her!

YOU CAN FIND MORE INFORMATION ON UPCOMING HARLEQUIN® TITLES, FREE EXCERPTS AND MORE AT WWW.HARLEQUIN.COM.

HPCNM0918RB

*Wary of being exploited for her fortune,
Athena is devastated to learn Alexios only wants her to
avenge himself against her father!
But when the consequence of their passion is
revealed, he wants her for so much more…*

Read on for a sneak preview of
Trish Morey's *next story*
Consequence of the Greek's Revenge.

"Going somewhere, Athena?"

Her breath hitched in her lungs as every nerve receptor in her body screeched in alarm. Alexios!

How did he know she was here?

She wouldn't turn around. She wouldn't look back, forcing herself to keep moving forward, her hand reaching for the door handle and escape, when his hand locked on her arm, a five-fingered manacle, and once again she tasted bile in her throat, reminding her of the day she'd thrown up outside his offices. The bitter taste of it incensed her, spinning her around.

"Let me go!" She tried to stay calm, to keep the rising panic from her voice. Because if he knew she was here, he must surely know why, and she was suddenly, terribly, afraid. His jaw was set, his eyes were unrepentant, and they scanned her now, as if looking for evidence, taking inventory of any changes. There weren't any, not that anyone else might notice, though she'd felt her jeans grow more snug just lately, the beginnings of a baby bump.

"We need to talk."

"No!" She twisted her arm, breaking free. "I've got nothing to say to you," she said, rubbing the place where his hand had been, still scorchingly hot like he had used a searing brand against her skin, rather than just his fingers.

"No?" His eyes flicked up to the brass plate near the door, to the name of the doctor in obstetrics. "You didn't think I might be interested to hear that you're pregnant with my child?"

Don't miss
Consequence of the Greek's Revenge,
available October 2018 wherever
Harlequin Presents® books and ebooks are sold.

www.Harlequin.com

HPEXP0918